the
PURLOINED
POODLE

the
PURLOINED
POODLE

Kevin Hearne

Horned Lark Press

This is a work of fiction. All of the characters, organizations, and events portrayed in these stories are either products of the author's imagination or are used fictitiously.

THE PURLOINED POODLE: OBERON'S MEATY MYSTERIES No. 1

A Horned Lark Press Book
Published by Horned Lark Press
1087-2482 Yonge Street
Toronto, ON M4P 2H5

www.hornedlarkpress.com

Reprinted Edition.
ISBN: 978-1-7382792-4-1

Interior Design and Formatting:
www.emtippettsbookdesigns.com

Printed in a Secret Volcano Lair by Antifascist Capybaras

By Kevin Hearne

www.kevinhearne.com

CHAPTER 1

The Boxer

Humans always miss the essential politeness of pugs. They see the smashed face, the eyes in a perpetual state of panic, and their tendency to freak out if you try to clip their toenails, but they don't understand why pugs get along so well with other dogs. It's the way their tails curl up and away from their asses, making them easy to sniff when you meet them for the first time. It's a great first impression. There's nothing more friendly than an easy-access back door.

In fact, the dogs you have to watch out for are the ones who *don't* want you to sniff their asses. That always means they're trying to hide something. And I say that because a good whiff of the back end tells you everything you really need to know about a hound. I've told Atticus this five billion or million or hundred times, I don't know which is right, but it's a lot. But even when he does his Druid thing and shape-shifts to hound form, he refuses to inhale the wealth of information found at the rear exit of any dog we might meet, and that makes no sense. He's got the same filters in his hound nose that I have that keeps the stink from making you sick. Those are the filters that allow us to find out what else is going on in the stuff we smell, whether it's a fire hydrant or a tree or a French poodle's cute curly derriere. I guess he'll never get over his human prejudices about asses.

I shouldn't judge him, though. He gives me sausage and snacks and belly rubs, and it's not like I don't have prejudices either. I mean, for one thing, there's cats. For another, I think Chihuahuas are the clearest evidence we have for alien life on earth. And then any dog who tries to face me and won't let me check out his backside? Yeah, I think that's shadier than a walk in a cemetery.

I ran into one such shady customer at the Alton Baker Dog Park in Eugene, Oregon. We live in the Willamette National Forest now near the McKenzie River, but Atticus takes me into town every so often so I can see other dogs besides Orlaith, and he can get things like bad coffee and worse donuts—he calls them sugar bombs. He always buys a newspaper full of ads for luxury automobiles too, but he says he reads it for the articles.

Whenever I walk into a park all the other dogs are like hobbits saying, "It comes in *pints?*" because they've never seen a hound as big as me before. They either get real excited or real scared. Or real yippy, like some of the small breeds who don't think I should be allowed. Yorkshire terriers don't care. They bark at me every time.

Boxers are all kinds of fun to play with, so I was excited to see one at the park. We usually get along great. I even passed by a pug who practically backed up to me by way of introduction to go meet the boxer. But this guy—I knew it was a guy because I could see from a distance he hadn't been neutered—growled at me when he thought I got too close. I wagged my tail and let my tongue hang out to let him know I was friendly. He still had his teeth bared and barked at me a couple of times to tell me to back off.

That's when I realized that this boxer wasn't playing with anyone else. He'd been standing alone by a spruce tree for a reason. I looked around to see if I could spot his human, but no one seemed particularly interested. Atticus was sitting on a bench reading his newspaper full of disasters. There were some other humans scattered about, some standing alone and one couple, but none of them were paying any attention to the others except for the couple. They were in conversation, the man talking and the woman looking concerned. Everyone else had their arms crossed and were all looking at their dogs, making sure they didn't get into any fights. Except no one was looking at me and the boxer.

I didn't want to fight. I wanted to play. I lowered my front half and kept my tail in the air, wagging, a clear signal that I was friendly and just wanted a chase. I woofed at him, nice as could be. But the boxer was kind of like Tybalt, this Prince of Cats Atticus was telling me about. A duelist looking for an excuse. His hackles raised and his growl got meaner, showing me teeth. That wasn't right. It was such a nice day.

<Hey, uh, Atticus?> I called to my Druid through our mental link. His voice answered in my head.

What is it, Oberon? I'm trying to read.

<Oh, well, I don't want you to stop your very important lounging. I just wanted you to know I might be getting into a fight here.>

Please don't. Just walk away.

<Yyyeahhh. That might not be an option.>

And it wasn't. The boxer lowered his head and charged. If I tried to run he'd have a shot at my legs. But my head was already as low as it could go—he didn't have a shot at my throat. I had one at his, though, and probably thirty pounds on him. So I wasn't scared. Not even a little. I mean, it's a bona fide, certified fact that I am hashtag-blessed in the fighting department. Because I'm an old dog who's learned plenty of tricks that my faithful Druid taught me.

I lunged up to meet his charge but kept my head down, butting him right in the nose with the crown of my head. Nothing for his teeth to chomp onto, really, and it stunned him, got rid of all that momentum. It also left him wide open for a swipe across his muzzle. That woke him up and he remembered he was a boxer and supposed to be good at this. He *was* good at it; he raked me with his claws a couple times, got a chomp on my shoulder when he couldn't get my neck, but I gave as good as I got. In fact, I recognized his pattern of attack and used a move that Atticus taught me, some kind of martial arts thing modified for hounds. The principles remained the same: Redirect your opponent's force to defend yourself and defeat him. So when he raised his right leg and came at me with a haymaker, I lunged inside of it, brought my left up underneath his shoulder, trapping his leg in the raised position, and just fell over to my right, taking him with me in a body slam—except that he went down first, and his throat was right underneath my jaws. He struggled and I clamped down a bit to let him know I was serious.

Atticus got into his head after a few more seconds and he calmed down, going still. I let him go and backed away as Atticus and the couple came running. Other humans were calling their tiny hounds and going home, worried that their pets would become collateral damage.

The boxer had some scratches, maybe some tiny teeth marks, and I had the same. No big deal. But worried people always take their time reaching the same conclusion. They need a nice healthy panic first.

The woman was a blonde of the chemical kind. Atticus told me one easy way to spot them was to look to see if the eyebrows matched the hair and hers weren't even close. I wondered if maybe she had a wig on. I think her skin was tan or maybe she was a darker-skinned human—I have trouble telling the difference because hounds don't see the same colors humans do. We can see yellow and blue and hints of other things, but most of it is shades of gray, especially the stuff between red and green. I had a hard time figuring out why Atticus insisted that a red ball—a dark gray to me—was a different color than the green grass it rested on, which was almost identical to my eyes. She had on running shoes that looked way too clean and tight dark leggings with a bright blue stripe on the calf. I'm not sure what the leg stripes signify—it's something I see more of lately. I know when humans have yellow stripes on their shoulders it sometimes means military rank, but maybe this leg stripe means she's super-fast compared to other humans. She was certainly faster than the dude she'd been talking to, and she smelled like lemons and dead flowers in that artificial soapy kind of way, plus a whiff of those vegetable dog snacks that Atticus calls "hipster doggie chow." Yuck.

The guy she outpaced huffed a bit, straining to keep up, and he shouted something that sounded like "algae" and then "stop," but that made no sense at all because we'd already stopped. That couldn't be the boxer's name, could it? Who would name their hound after stuff that scums up the surface of ponds and swimming pools?

He was kind of pale and dark-haired, his cheeks all blotchy from excitement or anger or some weird human disease, I don't know. But I liked him already, because he wore a T-shirt that said "Remember the Cant," a reference to a science fiction show on TV called *The Expanse*, and he smelled like real sausage and a continuing struggle with foot odor that he was losing. He and the woman scowled at me—they clearly thought I was a bad dog—and then huddled around the boxer as Atticus came over to check me out.

Ah. You'll be fine.

<I know.>

So what happened?

<I just wanted a friendly chase, Atticus, honest! But he rolled a twenty on his aggro and came after me. That's a seriously disturbed pooch. I'm not saying he's rabid or anything, just liable to snap at any moment, like Jack Nicholson in every movie ever.> Atticus looked doubtful so I had to press him. <Do your spooky Druid thing and check if you don't believe me! I know you calmed him down but that doesn't mean you got rid of his issues, right?>

Atticus shifted his eyes to the boxer while he petted me, and after a few hours or minutes or whatever it was he said, *You're right. He's upset about something.*

My human turned to face the couple and said, "I think they'll be all right. Nothing a bath won't fix."

"Yes, I'm sure," the man said. "Did you see what started it?"

"My hound wanted to play and I guess your hound wasn't in the mood."

"Ahh. Not surprising. Algy's been temperamental lately."

<Atticus, is he calling his boxer algae?>

Yes, but not what you're thinking. It's short for the British name Algernon.

"I'm sorry to hear that," Atticus said. "Any ideas about what might be bothering him?"

"Well, it's like I was telling her—oh, I'm sorry. This is Tracie Chasseur, and I'm Earnest Goggins-Smythe."

"Pleasure. I'm Connor Molloy," Atticus said, because that's the name he was using then. He goes through names the way I go through chew toys. "Chasseur? Is that Swiss?"

"It's eighteenth-century French Huguenot," the woman said, an edge to her voice that suggested she was offended. Maybe she didn't like being mistaken for Swiss. Or maybe she just didn't like Atticus. That happened sometimes. I mean, I've seen people try to kill him before they even say hello, which I'm pretty sure is impolite among humans if not outright rude. He just has that effect on some folks.

"Right, as I was telling her," Earnest said, "Algy was shot with a tranquilizer the night that Jack was abducted, and ever since he's been irritable."

"Wait—who was abducted?"

"My Grand Champion standard poodle, Jack. And he's not the first Grand Champion to be kidnapped—dognapped, whatever—in this area."

Tracie shook her head and crossed her arms. "I can't believe it's happening. They'd better not come after my English setters." I turned my head around to search for her hounds. I hadn't seen any English setters when I came in—ah, there they were. Feather-coated white hounds with blue belton markings playing around with a black lab in the opposite corner of the park, with one nervous human looking on. "If your wolfhound there is a Grand Champion I'd be careful."

"Oh, no, he's not," Atticus said.

<Hey! I can beat anybody!>

I know, Oberon. I'll explain later.

"Beautiful hound, though," Tracie said, and I decided I could forgive her for smelling like lemons. She'd have to do a lot more than flatter me to make up for the vegetable snacks she fed her hounds though. That was borderline cruelty. But even more cruel was to be separated from one's poodle. I wanted to know more about Earnest's tragedy.

<Atticus, will you ask him for details on that missing poodle of his?>

"Tell me more about what happened to your poodle, Earnest," Atticus said. "You said his name was Jack?"

"Yes. His full name is Jack Frederick Oscar Worthing Chasuble Wilde."

"Oh!" Atticus gave a smile and a little laugh, which he always did when he was trying to be charming. "I see you're an Oscar Wilde fan."

"Lots of guys named Earnest hate him, but I like him."

"So your boxer, Algernon, is named…?"

"Algernon Oscar Bunbury Moncrieff Wilde."

Dang, no wonder he shortened it to Algy. <Atticus, what's all this?>

Their names are mashups of characters from Oscar Wilde's play, The Importance of Being Earnest. *You have to have really long names to be registered with the AKC.*

<I don't know what the AKC is, but does that mean I can have a bunch of names too? Not just Sir Oberon Snackworthy?>

Knock yourself out.

<Sir Oberon Snackworthy del Sausage Gravy von Bacon Slab-O'Boeuf!>

You mean Slab-O'Beef?

<No, I mean *Boeuf.* It's like that Tracie lady's name. Eighteenth-century French Huguenot.>

But you're Irish.

<That's why it's *O'Boeuf* instead of just *Boeuf.* It's *fancy* Irish, Atticus.>

Oberon, do you even know what a Huguenot is?

I ventured a guess based on what the word kind of sounded like. <Like an astronaut but, uh…huge?>

I got a mental snort for that so I must have guessed wrong. And then I had to catch up with his conversation with Earnest. Atticus has this ability to use different headspaces when he wants, which I don't really understand except it means he can talk to me mentally while carrying on a different conversation with someone else.

"Is Algy a Grand Champion too?" Atticus was saying.

"Oh, no, he's just a love." Earnest smiled fondly at his hound and rubbed his head. "Traumatized, but strangely content at the moment."

He did look content sitting there, his tongue lolling out and all the aggression gone from his muscles. That was because he had a Druid in his head and that can be relaxing.

"So whoever pulled this off came prepared for Algy there. They wanted your poodle—but just because he's a poodle or because he's a Grand Champion?"

"I think it's the Grand Champion title, because of the rash of abductions we've had recently."

"This is happening a lot?"

"All throughout the Pacific Northwest," Tracie said, then looked at Earnest with a frown. "It started with Julia Garcia's Italian greyhound up in Tacoma, didn't it?"

"No, she was second," Earnest corrected her. "First was Ted Lumbergh's Brittany spaniel out in Bend."

"Oh yeah, I forgot."

"And after them went the French bulldog way up in Bellingham, and the Airedale terrier in Hillsboro. Then Jack was next."

"Incredible," Atticus said. "Are the police on this at all?"

Earnest shrugged. "We've tried to get them involved, but it's pretty clear that they don't care much. They don't even think it's the same person doing it. They think they just ran away, because dogs do that. Except these aren't somebody's rowdy mutts. They're Grand Champions, the most highly trained, pampered hounds in the world. And the fact that Algy got shot with a tranquilizer dart is pretty big clue that someone besides me was involved in the whole thing. It's probably how they did everything—shoot the dog and lay him or her out, then there's little or no barking, no owner woken up, and it's all done quiet and in the dark."

"Wow. But why?"

"Only reason I can think of is breeding. It's not someone trying to eliminate their competition in the shows or it would be the same breed every time. Someone is just after the money."

"I'm sorry, I don't understand. What money?"

"Grand Champions command top dollar in stud fees, so if you have a few of them, you can make a decent living, I suppose."

<What are stud fees, Atticus?>

If somebody has a bitch and they want her to have the best puppies possible, they pay someone else who has an excellent hound to come over and get her pregnant. That's a stud fee.

<Whoa. Whoa. Wait. You mean that I, as the most excellent hound ever in the history of the world, could get *paid* to hump bitches?>

No, I would be the one who gets paid. But it doesn't matter because we're not going to do that.

<We're not?>

Definitely not. I disagree with the ethics there.

<Oh. There are ethics there? Like an entire field of study about ethics in humping?>

Yes. And besides, you have Orlaith to consider.

<That's true!> As soon as I said it I realized it was only sort of true. Hounds aren't monogamous like most humans are. We don't get married or even think about committed relationships, which makes a lot of human dramas pretty silly to me. But Orlaith is the only other hound in the world I can talk to, which makes her special, and I think it would be rude to hump this deerhound or that Great Dane while she's pregnant with our puppies. <I would have remembered that in another decade or century or second or whatever! It just rocked my world to find out that this is a thing that happens.>

"How did you hear about all these other abductions?" Atticus asked.

"Oh, we have a bulletin board," Tracie said. "Or an online forum or whatever you call it. All the owners and trainers who go to shows in this region are on there."

"Ah, gotcha. So maybe that's how you're being targeted?"

Tracie and Earnest looked at each other with slightly widened eyes which in humans means that they are either surprised or something happened in their pants.

"Could be," Earnest admitted.

"But how would someone know who has a Grand Champion hound?" Atticus said.

Earnest closed his eyes—no, he squeezed them shut really hard and kinda made a growly face that showed some of his teeth. Atticus says that's called a wince. Which, now that I think of it, could also mean that something happened in Earnest's pants, but it probably meant he was doing one of those oh-god-I-am-such-an-idiot speeches inside his head.

"We have little stars by our names. And our biographies list it, without fail. It's an ego thing. We're proud."

"Shit," Tracie said. "That probably *is* how they're finding us. I should get rid of my star and rewrite my bio."

"But if that's true, Tracie, you know what that means?" Earnest said. "Whoever's doing this is one of us. A trainer, I mean. An expert with hounds."

"Shit, shit, shit," she said. "I gotta go change my profile thingie right now. Sorry." She glanced quickly at Atticus. "Nice to meet you, Connor. Maybe I'll see you here again." Then she took off after her hounds, calling, "Lizzie! Mr. Darcy!" and Atticus made a tiny sound of amusement.

<What's funny?>

Those names are from Pride & Prejudice *by Jane Austen.*

<Oh! You mean that movie with the Irish wolfhound in it living with the Bennets?>

Yes, the Keira Knightley version. But it was a book first. I like these people who name their hounds after literary characters.

<Like me, right? You named me after that guy in Shakespeare's play.>

That's right. He turned back to the man and his boxer.

"How many people do you think are on this bulletin board, Earnest?"

"A couple hundred, maybe? I'll have to check. I mean I definitely will. This is something I can share with the police. Thanks."

"Not a problem. Do you mind me asking—out of those couple hundred, how many of them are owners of Grand Champions?"

"Oh, only fifty or so, at most."

"That's a fairly large pool of targets. These abductions could go on for some time."

"God, I guess so."

"Listen," Atticus said, "I have a friend on the police force here in Eugene, a detective."

Ha! That was a lie. Atticus and the police did not get along. But Earnest didn't know that.

"Really?" he said. "Not Detective Callaghan?"

"Yeah!" Atticus gushed. "How do you...?"

"He's the one working Jack's case. If you can call what he's doing working. He doesn't seem to have much interest in it."

"Well, maybe I can do something about that. Would you mind telling me the address of this bulletin board? And giving me the names of the other victims? All I got was Julia Garcia and Ted Lumbergh."

The web address was a bunch of gibberish to me, but I did catch that the French bulldog's human in Bellingham was named Delilah Pierce, and the Airedale terrier's human in Hillsboro was Gordon Petrie.

"Thanks," Atticus said. "So let's say I'm a schmoe who's just stolen a Grand Champion stud. Or five of them. How do I turn that into a profit? Do I place ads online or in newspapers?"

"Oh, I've been looking for stud advertisements around here, believe me," Earnest said. "Nothing so far."

"Just around here? Not nationally?"

"Well, how would you figure out which one is my Jack? The number of poodle studs out there is huge. I'd have to check each one in person to see if it's really Jack, and that's not feasible."

"Got it. So whoever's doing this is probably shipping the hounds out of the region and turning them into money machines elsewhere."

Earnest deflated. "Most likely. He could be anywhere by now."

"Well, we have an idea of where to start. We have a five specific breeds to look for, so that gives us a search pattern. We might be able to narrow things down since so much is online and searchable now. And we have a pool of potential suspects on your bulletin board."

"I guess we do, huh?"

"Have some hope, there. I'll talk to the detective and see what we can do."

"Yeah? Hey, thanks, Connor."

"No problem."

They traded phone numbers and shook hands and then Atticus said goodbye. I hoped Algernon would be in a better mood if we ever met again. But I understood why he was upset: I know I'd be pretty wrecked if someone took Orlaith. She was always off with Granuaile in Poland and other places these days, pregnant with our puppies, and though she always came back eventually, I missed her something awful while she was gone. It was so much fun to have another hound to talk to as well as play with. I knew Atticus had gotten into the habit of bringing me to the dog park to take my mind off her and enjoy playing with other hounds, but that was only like a week or something out of every day.

"Come on, Oberon," he said, walking toward the tree we used to shift in.

<Hey, we're not going to shift out of here right in front of them, are we?> I asked, trotting after him.

Of course not. We'll make sure no one's looking.

<Are we going to look for Jack? Because I think we should. Algy's pretty sad without his friend and I guess Earnest is too.>

I was going to ask you about that. Technically it's none of our business.

<Nonsense! Wherever there's injustice it's our business!>

That would make most of the world our business, Oberon.

<Don't throw vague math terms like "most" at me! Here's the injustice we know about: A Grand Champion poodle has been stolen—a poodle who could sire more poodles—and nobody cares but his human! When the police don't act, it's our job to act in their stead!>

That's not actually our job.

<Well, what else are we going to do with our time while Orlaith and Clever Girl are in Poland? We can't be scrubs, Atticus! It's our duty to behave like we just read a self-help slogan! We have to be the change we want to see in the world!>

That's Mahatma Gandhi you're paraphrasing there, not a self-help guru.

<Whatever! You're focusing on the details instead of the big picture, and the point is that we have to help because we can!>

All right, I'm with you. I just want you to understand this might take a bit of work. It's not like television. You might get bored.

<No way! I've always wanted to be a detective!>

Yes, I've heard you say so on more than one occasion. But it's always in response to a show you just watched, and it's not going to be like that, where everything gets wrapped up nicely in an hour. Lab results won't conveniently come back in a few minutes—not that we'll have a lab to begin with. We won't have access to police records or equipment or any legal authority. We might not get anywhere with this.

<Are you trying to depress me right now? I'm getting nothing but negativity here.>

No, that's not what I'm doing. I'm trying to manage your expectations. I do want to try because I don't like the idea of someone possibly abusing those hounds.

<What?! Who could ever abuse a poodle?>

Atticus shrugged. *It's possible. Humans are capable of terrible stuff.*

<Like putting mustard on things?>

Yes, and even worse than that. Whatever the situation is, I'm sure Jack and these others are not as happy as they were with their owners.

<Well now we just have to find them. We *have* to! The game is afoot, Atticus!>

CHAPTER 2

The Man with the Big Salami

When I first heard the phrase "the game is afoot" in a *Sherlock* episode, Atticus had to explain both to me and his Archdruid Owen that it didn't mean the game was *a* foot, because that didn't seem like much of a game to either of us.

"How do ye make a game out of a fecking foot?" the Archdruid groused. "Doesn't it just stand there growing toenails? Or are ye supposed to dodge when it tries to kick ye?"

Atticus said it was a metaphor. If the game was catching the bad guy, and it was afoot, then it was moving, the criminal was getting away, and we had to get moving too if we wanted to catch him.

<First thing we need to do is interview the other people who had their hounds kidnapped, right?>

Right. So we need to go home first. I have to look up their addresses and then we can get started.

We arrived at the tree we used to shift in, and Atticus looked all around to see if anyone was watching us. When he put his hand on the trunk of the bound tree, I reared up on my hind legs and put one paw on the tree and the other on his shoulder. He shifted us to Tir na nÓg, the Fae plane that connects to everything, and then to our new place in the Willamette National Forest, where he had a bound tree next to the McKenzie River. We sprang up the steps to the backyard deck and then through the door. Atticus went straight to a laptop and I went straight for the water. For some reason he always wanted me to drink from the bowl instead of the river. He was afraid I'd get sick from some kind of bacteria in the water, but I'd taken a few drinks anyway when he wasn't looking. It was super cold and refreshing and I didn't get sick so I didn't see what the problem was, but I was going to follow procedure this time. When you're detecting you have to follow procedure. Unless you're a rogue cop like the ones on television, which usually means you also have substance abuse problems and marital troubles and get suspended a lot.

When I was finished hydrating, Atticus was almost finished looking up addresses. He had some kind of map displayed on his screen, which I didn't really understand how to read, but he absorbs things like that really well and doesn't have to print things out or write them down, just like I don't have to write down a smell if I want to remember it later.

"Okay," he said aloud, which he liked to do whenever it was just the two of us. "I know where to go. We'll have to jog around a little bit like always, but nothing terribly long. We'll visit them in order of abduction. Remember that these are all dog owners who might have additional dogs. They have high standards of behavior regarding hounds, so I'll need you to display your best manners. No leg humping or peeing on their property."

<Great big bears, Atticus, I know that by now!>

"Reminders don't hurt."

<But they sure can annoy! Let me take this opportunity to remind you not to hump the victims' legs or pee on them either.>

"Point taken."

We shifted down to some evergreen trees near Bend, Oregon, which Atticus said was to the south, and it was just a tiny bit colder somehow. A squirrel chattered at us and normally I would have stopped right there and recited Ezekiel 25:17 to him like Jules did to Brett in *Pulp Fiction*, but we were on a mission and I didn't have the time to deliver The Full Jules.

Bend smelled like bread and rotten vegetables, so thank the gods of all good smells for whoever baked the bread. I passed so many hydrants and light posts without even stopping once because they were outside our mission parameters. I was determined to be an efficient hound detective because that poodle needed our help.

Ted Lumbergh's house turned out to be on the outskirts of town with a lot of land attached and a pond behind it. Atticus commented that this meant Mr. Lumbergh made his money doing something else besides training Brittany spaniels. But he certainly had plenty of them left—they were barking at us long before we made it to the front door.

Mr. Lumbergh answered the door looking like a collection of wrinkles, both on his skin and his clothes. He had ceased to care about laundry in a previous century. He had a scowl for Atticus at first but when he saw me sitting next to him his whole face changed and he completely ignored my Druid. This happens a lot because I'm very handsome. He smiled with dazzling white and even teeth that Atticus had taught me to recognize as dentures.

"Well, hello there," he said in a strained, raspy old voice. "Who might you be?"

"This is Oberon," Atticus said, and added his own name, but Mr. Lumbergh just talked right over him.

"Hello, Oberon! You're quite the wolfhound. I don't remember seeing you in any of the shows around here."

"He's not a show dog, just very well-trained," Atticus said. I wagged my tail but didn't move otherwise.

"Bah. What a waste," Mr. Lumbergh replied, keeping his eyes on me as he talked. "You could go far with a hound like that. I don't suppose you came here looking for a trainer? I'm semi-retired now, but I'd reconsider for a hound like Oberon."

"We're actually here about your Grand Champion that got abducted."

"Huh?" That tore his eyes away. "How do you know about that?"

"We were just talking to Earnest Goggins-Smythe in Eugene. His poodle, Jack, was taken earlier this week."

"That so? I hadn't heard. Damn shame." The wrinkles twisted and scrunched around his face as he tried to remember Atticus's name. "Who are you again?"

"Connor Molloy. An amateur investigator. The police aren't doing much so I'm doing what I can. Mind if I ask you what happened to your Brittany spaniel?"

Ted Lumbergh shrugged. "Sure, I'll tell you. It's quick enough. Is Oberon okay around other dogs?"

"Sure."

He waved us in. "Come on through to the backyard then."

His house was dimly lit and smelled of leather, dusty books, and dry salami. Not the typical Genovese variety, though: This was *ciauscolo* from the Marche region of Italy. If he shared that with his hounds, I would count Mr. Lumbergh among the finest of humans.

He led us past several rooms and a kitchen to a sliding glass door where I could see and hear several excited hounds. They were all barking and wagging their tails, and Mr. Lumbergh calmed them down with a few curt commands shouted through the glass. They were well-trained.

Go ahead and play with them, Oberon, Atticus told me privately as we followed Mr. Lumbergh out to the deck. *I'll fill you in when we're done.*

There were four Brittany spaniels wagging their tails, all cute and eager with their brown-spotted white coats and floppy ears, and as soon as I cleared the door I darted to the right, where there were stairs leading down to an expansive lawn, and their toenails on the wood scratched and scrabbled to follow after. Once I hit the lawn, the race was on. It was fine Bermuda grass for a while then untamed scrub grasses around the pond, and right then nothing sounded so good as a nice course around the water feature. I gave the legs a good stretch—longer legs than any spaniel—and dared Mr. Lumbergh's hounds to catch me. They didn't have a prayer because Irish wolfhounds were bred to hunt down deer and actual wolves. We're fast and have mad stamina.

"Ha haaah! Lookit 'em go!" Mr. Lumbergh crowed as his hounds barked and pursued me. They had a pretty good deal here, I thought. Lots of room to run and stuff to smell, the occasional pair of birds to scare up here and there. They might even get deer or elk running through here sometimes, because there were some woods beyond the pond and nothing else I could see; Mr. Lumbergh's property was either extensive or backed up to forest land. I wondered how his hound had been stolen among all these others. Were they all tranquilized with darts? Or maybe sent to sleep by some tainted meat thrown over the fence? Humans liked to take advantage of our hunger sometimes. Atticus saved me from a poisoned steak once.

When I got to the far side of the pond, I stopped and turned, barked a couple of times in a friendly hello, and waited for the spaniels to catch up. We introduced our noses to one another's asses then and confirmed that we were all friendly doggies with privileged access to fine meats thanks to our humans. I wished I could ask them questions the way Atticus was asking Mr. Lumbergh, but they didn't know any language yet beyond a few training words, and they might not know anything more than Algy did about Jack's abduction if they were tranquilized. We played and nipped at each other for a few minutes until Atticus called me back.

"Oberon! Let's go!" he shouted, and I took off, letting the spaniels trail after.

<Find out anything good?> I asked him as I approached the deck, and his answer returned through our mental bond.

Hound's name was Ulysses. He wore a different collar than the rest of these others which made him easy to identify. They were fed some drugged snacks and Ted says whoever did it must know dogs pretty well, might even have some decent veterinary knowledge. Our theory about the thief being a member of that bulletin board community is probably a good one.

<So they weren't shot with darts?>

No. Earnest either didn't know that detail about this abduction or forgot to tell us.

<Does Mr. Lumbergh suspect anybody in particular?>

Sadly not. He doesn't post on the board all that often and can't think of anyone who'd have it in for him.

When Mr. Lumbergh asked if he could give me a slice of that *ciauscolo* for being such a good hound, I was determined to find Ulysses for him if I could. Think of the size of the salami he would give me for that!

We all scrambled inside to the kitchen and Mr. Lumbergh pulled out a lovely salami and a cutting board. The Brittanys knew what was up: They all sat around him in a circle, tails wagging. *Ciauscolo* isn't a dry, hard salami, but soft and almost spreadable on crackers or bread once you remove the casing. And it's melt-in-your-mouth *delicious*—not that I would ever let meat hang around in my mouth long enough to melt! He cut five thick slices, removed the casing from each, and tossed one to every hound in turn. Oh, suffering cats, I sure do like being a detective!

CHAPTER 3

A Grisly (Not Gristly!) Discovery

The next person to interview was Julia Garcia in Tacoma with the Italian greyhound. I ignored so many interesting trees and fire hydrants on the way there only to find out that she wasn't home.

<Aww, dang it!>

Told you it wouldn't always be easy.

<Well, who's next? We should just keep going. Ulysses and Jack are depending on us, even if they don't know it yet!>

Delilah Pierce, who lives in a town called Bellingham. She had Grand Champion French bulldogs.

Bellingham turned out to be a leafy little place just a few miles south of the Canadian border. Atticus shifted us to a fresh-smelling forest surrounding Lake Padden. It had just finished raining when we got there, the ground all soft and springy underfoot. Delilah lived nearby in a big old house on Broad Street with vines creeping up the sides.

Her kids—a boy and a girl—promptly draped themselves all over me once Atticus assured them I was friendly. They smelled like marshmallows and stinky cheese. Delilah didn't want me in the house, though—not only was I kind of muddy, she had two more Frenchies in there, yapping away, and thought it would be best if we talked on the porch. She sent the boy in to fetch some drinks and we all sat down, I to be petted by the girl, and Atticus to interview Delilah. He smiled a lot and did his charming human thing, telling her about Ted and Earnest and how he was trying to track down what happened to all the abducted hounds.

"Are you with law enforcement?"

"I'm a private investigator," Atticus said, laying down a lie slicker than a polished marble floor. "Earnest hired me."

Atticus found out that all her Frenchies had been drugged to sleep just like Ted Lumbergh's down in Bend, and I thought that was interesting. Why had Earnest's boxer been shot with a tranquilizer dart instead? Were we dealing with two different criminals, or the same one that recently decided to up their game? That might have been a mistake though. Dart guns had to be traceable, didn't they, as well as tranquilizers capable of being injected that way? I'm pretty sure you can't go to the supermarket and pick up some nice liquid animal tranquilizers. You have to get them from a veterinarian. But I'd have to ask Atticus to confirm all that. It seemed to me that spiking treats would be much tougher to trace back to a perpetrator because the evidence quite literally turned to poo.

I lost some bits of their conversation after that because the boy returned, delivered cans of soda to the big people, asked Atticus if he could feed me, and then came over with a bag of snacks. They were peanut butter bombs and the kids giggled their heads off as I licked my chops at the sticky stuff. Infuriating food, peanut butter. Can't say no to it, and yet it's so difficult to eat.

Atticus turned his line of questioning to what the dog trainers' online forum was like and if she posted often and I tuned some of that out, but I heard him ask, "Has anybody stopped posting all of a sudden?" and that sounded interesting. Delilah's answer definitely was.

"Well, yes," she said, "I'm a bit worried, in fact. There's a friend of mine who lives down in Portland who has Boston terriers—they're so similar to Frenchies that we see each other at shows quite often. She posted most every day but hasn't for the past couple, and I texted her a few hours ago and she hasn't replied. I know that there could be all sorts of rational explanations—she's on a cruise, she lost her phone, or any number of things—but she's a bit older, you know, and living alone, so I worry."

"What's her name?"

"Verity Boone-Sutcliffe. Charming English lady who still takes her tea in the afternoon."

"And she has a Grand Champion Boston terrier?"

"Yes. Wickedly smart fellow."

"Does she have any others?"

"No, just the one dog."

"And like you—and Ted, Julia, and Earnest—she had this information about her dog publicly available on the forum?"

"Yes, she did." Her hand flew to her mouth. "Oh, now you have me really worried."

"Well, I'm heading down that way because our next stop is in Hillsboro—Gordon Petrie's Airedale, you know. Maybe I can just knock on her door and make sure she's okay?"

"If you do, will you let me know?"

"Of course. Might you have her address?"

We took our leave soon after that, me still trying to get peanut butter out of my mouth as we trotted back to Lake Padden. Atticus twisted his head around to make sure no one was in earshot, and then he talked to me out loud.

"Oberon, the timeline worries me here, so I want to go through it with you."

<Okay. Is this linear time or a big ball of wibbly-wobbly timey-wimey stuff?>

"Linear time. Each one of these abductions, after the first one, took place about four to six days apart. Jack was abducted about a week ago, right?"

<If you say so. I thought it was a month, which is seven days.>

"No, that's a week."

<Right! Right. I was just testing you.>

"Delilah just told us that she hasn't heard from Verity for two days. She has a Grand Champion Boston terrier. And two days ago would be five days after Jack was abducted."

<Oh! So you think she might be the next victim?>

"It's possible. Thought we might drop in on her next, like I said, instead of going to visit the guy in Hillsboro with the Airedale."

<That would be fine with me. Where is Portland again?>

"Close to Hillsboro, actually, in Oregon. They have a place there with maple bacon donuts if you want one."

<That sounds better than peanut butter right now. But ehhh, maybe not something so sugary. I would like something with gravy in it.>

We shifted out of Bellingham and into Peninsula Park in Portland, which had the distinction of being particularly rosy. We came out next to an old linden tree with mossy, gnarly roots, near a bandstand that faced a huge open field on one side and a huge rose garden and a fountain on the other. The fountain was in the middle of a shallow pool that little kids were splashing about in and shrieking happily. It looked inviting and I wanted to go in there and play a bit, maybe see if there were any rabbits hiding in the bushes, but Atticus said that if I didn't freak out the kids, I'd freak out their parents because I was supposed to be on a leash.

<But I'm a friendly hound, Atticus. And very handsome too.>

They won't know that immediately.

<Well let me at least smell some stuff. What's the hurry?>

Do you want to find those kidnapped hounds or not?

<Oh, yeah! Thanks for reminding me! Let's go.>

Sometimes when the opportunity to play presents itself, I forget what I'm supposed to be doing. Atticus says that means I'm squirrelly and almost hurts my feelings. I don't think that word means what he thinks it means. I am nothing like a squirrel.

Atticus said we had to go through town a bit to get to the address Delilah Pierce gave us for Verity Boone-Sutcliffe. And he wanted a coffee anyway. So we jogged south on a street called Albina for a while and turned left on Alberta, which Atticus claimed would lead him to coffee and me to a meat pie.

<What kind of meat pie?>

You'll see. When we get to Northeast 18th, there's a place called Random Order Pie Bar. They have mostly sweet pies, but I'm guessing you'll like the savory ones with gravy in them. And I can get a pretty decent flat white across the street.

I snerked at him. I'd heard this flat white business before. <But not as good as you'd get in Australia or New Zealand, right?>

Right. Atticus likes to give himself little culinary quests. Always looking for flat whites like they have Down Under, or ramen like you can get in Japan, or when he's overseas, he looks for tacos and barbecue like you get in the Americas.

I thought of a terrible pun and that was usually good for an extra snack so I said to Atticus, <Hey, if you can make milk from any mammal and the Australian platypus nurses its young, does that mean you could get a *plat* white?>

He groaned and promised me a bonus sausage later. Victory!

The pie bar had a chicken pot pie ready to go and the gravy in it was perfect—so good that it disguised the taste of vegetables in there! And Atticus turned out to be highly amused by the "authentic, free-range, organic yogurt-fed hipster" who made him his flat white. The barista had the oiled beard and thick black glasses going on, the flannel shirt, the skinny jeans and everything—maybe even a liberal arts degree, Atticus said. I love it when he does that—notice things aloud, or in my head, while we're eating. I learn things and it's delicious, and I know he's doing it on purpose so that I associate learning with food, but I don't care. It's our thing and it's fun. And afterward it makes me notice more than just what I can smell, which is probably a good thing when you're trying to solve a dastardly crime.

Fortified by gravy and coffee and already liking the city, we continued south on NE 18th Avenue toward the Irvington neighborhood. The houses were all different, unlike what I used to see in Arizona, where you saw neighborhoods with the same few models repeated with only minor variations, and that was mostly the plants they had to pee on in the front yard. These Portland houses were built nineteen thousand centuries ago, I think, because Atticus said they were built in the nineteen hundreds to the nineteen-teens. He told me that they were mostly Craftsman homes, full of interesting quirks and additions built in later epochs. They had mature trees towering over the houses, big porches wrapping around them, and quite a few of the properties had cement or stone retaining walls around an elevated lawn, and moss grew on them and even on the steps leading up to the houses. Whole lot of moisture there, Atticus explained, and it did feel like it was going to rain soon. Lots of pride in the homeowners, too, though, if their immaculate lawns were any measure. Moss was allowed to flourish on the outsides of the retaining walls, but no one could bear an unkempt patch of turf. Maybe they had a really serious HOA, like that one episode of the *X-Files* where a monster ate you if you violated the CC&Rs.

We turned left down Tillamook—a name I noticed because it's a brand of cheese Atticus buys sometimes—and then right on NE 24th. "Okay, Oberon," Atticus said, stopping in front of a two-story pale blue house with strips of white wood doing architectural things I don't know the name of. They were decorative and attractive patterns to humans, I guess. The glass in a couple of the windows was strange and I asked Atticus about it.

"That's leaded glass. Stained some colors you can't see. A bit hoity, maybe even toity. All right, plant quiz time. You should know all of these. There's a grilled bratwurst in it for you if you get them all right. No mustard, just the way you like it. Go."

Atticus had been teaching me the names of different plants recently instead of simply letting me pee on them. I'm not sure why—I announced once that I just peed on an oleander, thinking he'd congratulate me, but he said I didn't need to share that.

<All, right, uh, this hedge along the front here is boxwood. Sometimes you can find hedgehogs and lizards in those.>

"Excellent. And those big suckers in the flower bed along the porch?"

<Uh, that's…rhodo-dodo-dentition?>

"Rhododendron. That was close enough to count. The bratwurst could still be yours. What are those plants with the long stems and puffy explosion of flowers at the end, kind of like lavender Q-Tips?"

<Hydration!> As soon as I said it, I knew it was wrong. Atticus shook his head and my ears fell.

"You got the first part right. Want a second chance, or do you want to settle for kibble for dinner?"

<Well, yeah, I want a second chance! There's *meat* on the line here! Okay. First part was right. Hydra. Hail Hydra! But a different ending. Oh! I remember now! *Hydrangea!*>

Atticus scratched me behind the ears and smiled. "That's right. Smart hound. Brats for dinner tonight. Okay, it's nose time. I want you to go first up to the door, trying to pick up everything you can, and then if something turns out to be amiss, maybe we'll be able to attach those smells to something later. We don't want to contaminate what's there by walking all over it first."

<Got it. Collect the evidence and classify it, and after we smoke a lot of pipes like Sherlock Holmes, we'll put it together in a moment of revelation that has a German word I forget right now.>

"I think the word you want is *gestalt*."

<That's it! Do I still get a snack for remembering it was German?>

"Let's talk about sirloins instead of snacks if we can solve this. Take your time, file everything away. It might be important."

Sirloins, plural, are some of the world's most powerful motivators. It provides me a clarity and purpose like almost nothing else. I'm not really a scent hound, I'm more of a sight hound when it comes to hunting, but that doesn't mean I can't tell a cheesesteak from roast beef. So I put my nose to the narrow concrete walk and paced up to the porch steps, where we heard a dog begin to bark inside—the Boston terrier, no doubt.

"Oh, that's a relief," Atticus said. "If the Boston's here, then he obviously hasn't been abducted."

<So she's probably okay?>

"Yes, but we'll go ahead and knock just to make sure, and tell her Delilah is worried about her."

He stepped past me, no longer worried about contaminating smells, and rapped smartly on the door, sending the Boston into a frenzy inside.

"Ms. Boone-Sutcliffe?" Atticus called. "I'm just checking to make sure you're okay. You don't even have to open the door. Delilah Pierce in Washington is worried about you. Just tell me you're all right and I'll be on my way. Maybe give her a call."

The Boston continued to bark and nobody shushed him. No muffled voice called to say they were coming. Atticus knocked again. We got plenty more barking, but no human. I tried to come up with a harmless explanation.

<Maybe she's in the shower. Or out shopping. Or she's in the bathroom upstairs with a really big book, and she's right at the good part, you know, like you get sometimes with those thriller novels and you just disappear for an hour and I don't know where you went until you come out and complain your legs went to sleep on the toilet?>

Atticus switched to mental communication since the lady might come to the door and hear him. *Hmm. Maybe, buddy. But I'm more worried, not less. Can you smell anything through the door that seems wrong?*

I hadn't thought of trying that. I padded forward and snuffled at the door jamb, and then at the weather strip along the bottom. Something came through. Dog, of course, and tea and bacon and probably illegal amounts of cinnamon apple potpourri. But also decay.

<Oh, great big bears, Atticus, you might be right. Smells like something died in there.>

You're sure?

<Well, I'm sure something's dead. Doesn't mean it's the lady though. Could be a cat or a sasquatch or almost anything.>

Yeah, but Occam's Razor says it's probably the lady.

<*Whose* razor said that? Wait, back up—razors can *talk?*>

He didn't answer me but instead looked around to see if anyone was watching us. The street was quiet at the moment, no cars passing by, no joggers or bicyclists either.

I'm going to cast camouflage on us and break in just to check. I want you to stay near the door so you don't leave many traces. Try not to shed. This might be a crime scene.

<How do I not shed? I don't have control over each little hair on my body.>

Just think tidy thoughts. Or we might be tracked down by CSI: Portland.

<I never watched any of those shows. Are they good?>

No idea. But every city has a crime scene investigation unit. Actually, now that I think on it, I'm going to take the time to bind your hair to your body and mine as well. We definitely don't want to leave any traces here.

Atticus did a bunch of his Druid stuff then, speaking in Old Irish, which hardly anyone speaks anymore, to make things bind together that normally wouldn't behave that way. He smooshed my fur kinda flat all over my body, and his too. Then he cast camouflage, which had something to do with binding pigments to their surroundings, tricking the eye into seeing different colors and blurring outlines. That one takes a lot of energy to maintain so he doesn't like to do it for long, plus it kind of tickles whenever he does it to me. He was going to unlock the door by binding the tumblers to their unlocked positions, metal to metal, but he grunted in surprise and said it was already open. There were scratch marks around the keyhole.

Okay, here we go, he said. *Remember the Boston will be defending his home turf and might not be polite at first, so be patient with him until I can get him calmed down.*

<I think I can survive a Boston attack for a few years, Atticus,> I said. <I must outweigh him by three cows or something.>

You mean something like a hundred and twenty pounds. Cows are not a unit of measurement.

<They would be if hounds were running things.>

Just watch the teeth, all right? Bostons have very strong jaws and necks. It'll be tough to shake him off if he gets hold of something.

<Okay, I'll be careful.>

Atticus paused before opening the door, scanning the street one more time, and waited for a car to pass by so that they wouldn't see the door seem to open and close by itself. Once it was clear, he told me to move fast, and we slipped inside. Atticus dropped our camouflage as soon as the door closed, and the Boston was waiting. He barked once and flew right at my face, teeth bared. I turned my head, lifted a leg, and pawed him aside so that he missed and wound up with a mouthful of wooden floor. Undeterred, he scrambled back up to lunge again, and I had to use my other leg to slap him away twice more. That gave Atticus time to form a bond with him and calm him down. I don't know what he was saying mentally, but he spoke out loud, too, because it helped a little bit and let me know what was going on.

"Hey, hey, it's all right. We're here to make sure Verity is okay. We're not here to hurt her or you. Is she all right? Where's Verity?" He squatted down on his haunches, staring intently at the wee doggie, who truly did look like a prize specimen of the breed. Sleek black coat, milky socks on his paws and white fur on his chest, a sort of white racing stripe running down between the eyes and then spilling down either side of his nose, giving him white, whiskered chops that lacked all the slobber one normally gets from an English bulldog or a boxer.

The Boston sat down, ears laid back, and trembled all over. Poor little guy! He was scared. Atticus communed with him silently for a while, and it did take a bit longer than talking to me because the Boston probably only knew a few words and phrases like "sit" and "no" and "who's a good boy?" Atticus had to do everything through pictures and emotions and sort through it.

"Says his name's Starbuck," Atticus said finally.

<Starbuck? He's named after the *Battlestar Galactica* viper pilot?>

"No, I'm pretty sure he's named after the first mate of the *Pequod*. The Starbucks coffee chain is named after the same character."

<Whoa, whoa, whoa. You're blowing my mind here. You mean the Starbuck from *Moby Dick*?>

"That's the one. He was the first mate to Captain Ahab and pretty much the only character on the ship who gave a damn about animals and thought they were being cruel to the white whale."

<Yeah, I remember you telling me about him. Atticus, this can't be a coincidence! This is just like my story, the one I told you in Greece that one time!>

"Which story?"

<I told you a story called *The Purloined Poodle* and there was a Weimaraner named Ishmael investigating Abe Froman, the Sausage King of Chicago, along with the help of his trusty companion, a Boston terrier named Starbuck!>

"Well, that's…whoa."

<You remember now?>

"Yes, I do. The coincidence is kind of spooky."

<I am the Hound of Prophecy! Abe Froman must be behind this!>

"Let's not leap to conclusions yet. Starbuck thinks Verity's not well. He's very hungry and thirsty, says he hasn't been fed in a while, and his water bowl's dry."

<That's not good. Where is she?>

Atticus rose and peered across the room we were in, which I guessed would be called a parlor or sitting room, into the next one, which looked like it might be a kitchen. The old bacon smell came from there, but so did the decay. The source of the pungent cinnamon apple potpourri, unfortunately, was quite near the door on a fancy little table. It was in a decorative glass bowl to hold decorative smells for the infamously weak noses of humans.

"I'm going to go check on her," Atticus said. "Stay here with Starbuck, please. Make friends. Say hi to his ass for me."

I wagged my tail and did my best to look friendly to Starbuck, even though he must think I was way too big to be allowed in his home. Curiosity got the better of him and he gave me a couple of query sniffs before rising and moving to my back end. I let him go first, and then it was my turn. He did come across as stressed out and agitated but certainly not a mean fellow. And his wee belly growled with hunger. He needed a snack as soon as possible, or maybe half a cow would be better. I wished I could talk to him like I could to Orlaith and reassure him that food would be on the way soon, but unfortunately that wasn't possible. I'd be sure to remind Atticus that he was hungry though, because my Druid never lets his hounds go hungry like that.

Damn it, Atticus's voice cursed in my head. *She's dead, all right. And it wasn't natural causes, either.*

<How do you know?>

Because there's a tranquilizer dart sticking out of her left shoulder.

<She got killed by a tranquilizer?>

Not directly. She probably had a heart attack or some other reaction to the drug and that's what did it. Or else she just fell and cracked her head, but I don't see any blood.

<Can I come see? All my fur is still sticking to my body.>

Yeah, come on through to the kitchen.

I trotted in there, Starbuck trailing afterward, and found Atticus kneeling down in the kitchen next to the sprawled body of Verity Boone-Sutcliffe, who had thin, wispy white hair on her head and a pair of thick glasses all askew on her face. She was wearing a long white dress with blue flowers all over it and a black wool sweater on top, unbuttoned. No blood, like Atticus said—I couldn't see or smell any—so she'd broken her fall at least that much.

Her face had lots of age wrinkles in it but you could tell she had earned them from smiling instead of scowling. She was a bit chubby, as older humans get sometimes when they stop running like they used to when they were kids, but not hugely overweight. And just like Atticus said, she had a tranquilizer dart sticking up out of her left shoulder.

<Okay, so our naughty nemesis comes in to snatch Starbuck—maybe picks the lock—Verity surprises him, and then pow! He shoots her instead of the Boston. She falls down, and he takes off without the dog because, uh…well, I don't know. Why didn't he take Starbuck if she was down and out of the way?>

Atticus shrugged and said aloud, "Maybe he only had the one dart. Or maybe Starbuck attacked him. Maybe he just took off, especially if he knew he'd killed her. I don't think he expected to find Verity awake and walking around. But I do think you're right that this was done by the same person that kidnapped the other hounds. Your average burglar doesn't break and enter people's homes with a tranquilizer gun, and it doesn't appear that the place has been robbed or even searched. No, they came here after Starbuck, but Verity got shot instead, and her old heart couldn't take the strain. I don't think they intended to kill her, but she's dead all the same."

<So now what do we do?>

Atticus sighed. "That's a problem. We really should call the police and let them take care of this. But it's going to cause quite a bit of trouble for us if we do."

<Can't you just do one of those anonymous tip thingies?>

"I can, but then what's going to happen to Starbuck?"

<Well, we take him and feed him, of course. Or feed him first, which would be nicer, and then take him.>

"We can feed him now—I'll look for some chow right away. But if we take him, then *we* will be guilty of kidnapping."

<But we don't want to use him for humping fees!>

"Stud fees."

<Whatever it's called. We just want him to be a happy dog who gets fed on a regular basis.>

"The authorities wouldn't look at it that way. We broke in here, and if we take Starbuck and don't report the murder, then it's a crime."

<We didn't break in. The door was already open.>

"Oh—hey, that's right." Atticus clambered to his feet and started opening cupboards in the kitchen. He found a box of dog treats in one and tossed one each to me and Starbuck. There was also a smallish bag of high-end formula kibble in there, and he poured some into a bowl for Starbuck and then filled up his water dish as well. The Boston drank his fill first, then attacked the kibble. I shuddered at the horror of dry food and remembered that Atticus was going to make me a grilled bratwurst later. With Starbuck's needs taken care of for the moment, Atticus returned to the problem of what to do next.

"I think we'll call the police and then ask if we can take care of Starbuck until someone in Verity's family claims him. The problem will be the timeline."

<This is still linear time?>

"It is. See, we just met Earnest Goggins-Smythe and Algernon this morning. And then we talked to Ted Lumbergh in Bend and Delilah Pierce in Bellingham before coming here to Portland."

<So?>

"So we shouldn't have been able to do all that in one day. Especially the part where we said goodbye to Delilah Pierce in northern Washington and then discovered the body of Verity Boone-Sutcliffe less than an hour later in Portland."

<And an hour is how long again?>

"Sixty minutes."

<That sounds like a lot of minutes to me.>

"It's not enough, trust me. And I have to think about what to tell the police about who I am and what I do and why I'm snooping around in this affair."

<Well, if you need to look official, why don't you give them a business card? One that says you're a private investigator?>

"You need an actual license to be a private investigator. They'll check up on that and know I'm lying."

<So call yourself a consultant. Isn't that what people do when they want to get paid for knowing stuff?>

Atticus nodded. "That's not a bad idea. Wouldn't need a license to be a consultant. They would ask me what kind of consultant, though. Maybe I could call myself an animal rights advocate or something. And if I go get some cards made real quick, that would help with the timeline a tiny bit. I could cook up a story, print a card or two, then come back and call this in. It's not like she'll be *more* dead in an hour."

<Very good, Druid. Make it so.>

Atticus searched through the house and found several useful things. He found a framed Grand Champion certificate on the wall providing the full name of our new Boston terrier friend: "Verity's Boy From Nantucket Starbuck," which apparently confirmed for Atticus that he was named after the *Moby Dick* character and not the Viper pilot. And he found a collection of harnesses and leashes hanging on hooks in the hallway, which he promptly attached to me and Starbuck so that we could exit the house and prepare a cover story for the police.

We had to do this sort of thing often so I was used to it. Atticus couldn't just go around telling people the truth—that he was five billion years old or something like that, and he was a Druid who could shift planes via a network of trees rooted and bound to Gaia, the heart of all worlds. He specifically showed me *Terminator 2* to illustrate what would happen to him if he tried to tell the truth.

"See, Oberon?" he said. "If I tell people the truth about who I am and what I can do I'll wind up like Sarah Connor. Strapped down to a bed, injected with all kinds of chemicals, and random dudes licking my face for no reason. After that it's all explosions and massive property damage because uninvited lickings just make you want to burn the whole world down. So I have to lie."

We jogged south together until we got to Broadway, a street full of cars and businesses completely out of tune with the quiet neighborhood of Irvington. Atticus bought a new burner phone first and bought some minutes for it. Then he found one of those print shops and left me and Starbuck loosely tied up outside while he ducked in to create and print a few fraudulent business cards, putting his new phone number on them and charging his phone while he was at it. He was only gone for ten months or so and Starbuck and I enjoyed plenty of attention from people passing by.

Cards in hand, Atticus jogged with us back to the house and he called the police on his new phone—he still had his other one but he was keeping that off with the battery removed. He fetched a couple of snacks for us inside and then we waited together on the front porch.

He explained to the officers who arrived first that he'd been asked to look in on Verity by a friend, Delilah Pierce, discovered the door open, and found the body that way. He'd been very careful not to touch it or move anything, except to feed the dog and put him on a leash and wait outside.

The officers let us stay on the porch until a detective arrived, and then Atticus had to go over everything again. The detective flashed a badge at him as she took the steps in black leather boots and her eyes flickered at me, wondering if I was a threat or not. She had long dark hair and her lips were pretty dark too, though I didn't know if that meant they were red or actually some shade of black. Probably red because I think black lipstick was supposed to be a warning that the person was liable to be a cat person, though I might not be remembering that right. Her skin was kind of dark compared to Atticus's and she smelled like hot pepper sauce, which is not bad at all for a human. I've smelled much worse.

"Detective Gabriela Ibarra, Portland PD," she said. "Are you the man who called in the murder?"

"Yes," Atticus said. "Connor Molloy."

"Okay if I ask you a few questions, Connor?"

"Sure."

She flipped open a little note pad and clicked a pen. "How did you know the victim?"

"I didn't. I was asked to look in on her by a friend of hers in Washington, Delilah Pierce. She hadn't heard from her in a couple of days and got worried."

"How did you get in the house?"

"The door was open. I looked in when there was no answer but a barking dog. He sounded stressed."

"The dog sounded stressed?"

"Yes. I'm a trainer and an investigator of sorts."

"What kind of investigator?"

"May I give you my card?" He withdrew one of the cards he'd just printed and extended to her with two fingers. She took it and flicked her eyes down to the type. "Says here you're a dog trainer and animal rights advocate."

"That's right. I've been looking into a series of abductions throughout the Pacific Northwest."

"Dog abductions?"

"Yes. I'm worried that these animals are being abused. Delilah Pierce, Verity Boone-Sutcliffe inside, and other professional trainers on the same regional online forum have all lost AKC Grand Champions in recent months. Just last week, a man down in Eugene had his boxer shot with a tranquilizer like the one used on Ms. Boone-Sutcliffe."

"And the boxer was abducted?"

"No, he wasn't a Grand Champion. The standard poodle in the same house was, however, and the poodle was taken."

Atticus went through the facts with the detective and when she tried to zero in on when everything happened, exactly, he shrugged and got vague. "I don't know exactly," he said, and would say things like "Earlier," or "a while ago." She didn't like that very much, but at least she had a bunch of names to check out and that forum to investigate. And a solid motive to pursue: Some humans make money when they let their hounds get busy.

"Thank you," she said when he'd answered all her questions, and looked at his card again. "Is this number current if I need to reach you?"

"Yes. One question before you go. May I keep Starbuck with me until one of Ms. Boone-Sutcliffe's family comes forward to claim him? I'd rather he didn't suffer any more stress than he already has, and he's happy with my wolfhound."

Detective Ibarra looked at me and then at Starbuck, who was sitting right by my side, his tongue hanging out happily. "Sure, I don't see why not," she said, and extended a card of her own. "I'll be in touch, but please call if you turn up anything else."

"Will do."

We were free to go and Atticus took us south again toward the busy Broadway street.

<Aren't we going back to a park to shift out of here?> I asked him.

"We can't. I don't know Starbuck well enough yet to shift with him. If he were to lose some of his personality or memories because of my ignorance I'd feel terrible. It shouldn't take long to get to know him better, but I'm not there yet. So we have to go home the slow way. We have to actually rent a car."

<You mean a really big SUV I hope. I don't fit into most cars very well.>

"Maybe a midsize then."

Atticus reinserted the battery on his older phone, looked up a rental place with it, and we jogged over there. He let me and Starbuck stop and smell whatever we wanted and pee on it too because there was no hurry now. We were done investigating for the day and would resume in the morning.

Once on the road in some kind of SUV, me n' my new buddy Starbuck hung our heads out the rear window and let our tongues flap in the wind while Atticus called up Earnest Goggins-Smythe on his new phone and told him about Verity. He should expect a call from Detective Ibarra in Portland, and he should make sure to tell her that Detective Callaghan in Eugene was supposed to be looking into things too. And then he asked if he and Algy might be able to meet us sometime tomorrow in the same dog park where we'd met them that morning. "I might have some additional questions for you and maybe Algy and Oberon will get along a bit better this time now that they've been introduced. We'll keep an eye on them."

Earnest said he'd be around since he was a software developer and worked at home anyway, so he'd be able to meet us whenever we needed. That vague date made, we stopped in Eugene for a break, and he called Granuaile.

"Oh, good, you're home," he said. "Oberon and I have been adventuring today. We'll have a guest staying with us for a while. His name is Starbuck."

The road home from Eugene was sixty miles or something like that, Atticus said, but since it was kind of twisty and you had to go slow, it took longer to drive and it was past dark when we finally got home. Driving is so much slower than shifting planes. Starbuck and I curled up in the back seat and napped for most of it, I think, so we were ready for good times when we arrived at the homestead, and I got to introduce the wee doggie to Orlaith.

<Look, Orlaith, I got a lil' buddy! But his name's not Gilligan. It's Starbuck.>

<Oh my! What a cute little guy! I love how Bostons are all snorty and sneezy. Whoa, he's kind of excited, isn't he?> Starbuck was spinning around in circles and leaping up and down and barking cheerfully at Orlaith in front of the porch. She woofed back at him a couple times, and then they said hello more thoroughly by putting noses to asses. <Does he know his words yet?> Orlaith asked.

<Not yet. He knows some from his human training but hasn't had a Druid in his head until today. Atticus says he's really smart though.>

<Is he going to stay with us?>

<For a little while. His human was killed by another human, so we are going to be his family until his human's family comes to claim him.>

<Oh, how sad! He does smell like he was pretty stressed out recently.>

<Yeah, but that's nothing some good food and fun can't fix, right? Atticus promised to make bratwurst tonight!>

<He did? Granuaile promised me the same thing!>

<Sometimes I think they plan stuff like that just to make us happy.>

Our Druids had already gone inside, presumably to smooch and talk about human things, and hopefully get dinner going. They would call us when they wanted us. In the meantime, we could run around and play.

<Let's see how fast he can run!> Orlaith said, and with that we were coursing around the house, watching to see if Starbuck could keep up. Over the short term, he did—he's a fast little guy! But after a lap we pulled away, since Starbuck's lungs and legs weren't big enough to keep that up for very long. We didn't want him to feel left behind, so we pulled up and dodged around and tumbled and wrestled and so on. Eventually we all just lay down on some cool soft earth by the riverbank and panted and listened to the water gurgle past us.

<How are you feeling?> I asked Orlaith. She was just starting to show that she was pregnant.

<Pretty good!> she said. <But Granuaile says I will start to feel heavier and slower very soon and I probably shouldn't shift with her until after the puppies are born, so I'll be staying here with you and Atticus a lot more. And Starbuck, of course.>

<Well, hey, I'm all for that! We could use your help solving crimes!>

<What crimes?>

I got her caught up with our shenanigans while Atticus was no doubt doing the same thing with Granuaile, and eventually we got called in for bratwurst. Starbuck didn't know what was happening when we rocketed to our feet and sprinted for the back door, but he was happy to follow and see what we were suddenly excited about. We plowed through the extra-large doggie door and too late I worried if Starbuck could handle it, but it was no problem for him. It was bigger than he was used to but he had the strength to push through and wasn't afraid of the door at all.

"Oh! Atticus, he's adorable!" Clever Girl said when she saw him. "Starbuck! C'mere!"

The Boston went right up to her and snuffled her fingers and she got a few quick pets in before he got distracted by all the other things to smell in this new environment.

<Atticus, you'd better tell him not to pee on anything,> I said.

Already on it, buddy.

<Good. Wow, those brats smell good. You should tell Starbuck about the rules.>

Which rules?

<Mostly the one about never stealing my sausage.>

Oh, right. There's enough for everyone and never a need to wrangle over portions. Never fear.

It was a pretty good night because we saved a pooch in trouble. Starbuck got full on food that wasn't kibble and so did we, and Atticus gave all of us some kind of Druid tea to help out with the issues dogs have sometimes when they eat a lot of high-fat meat. And in the morning we would wake up, continue our investigation, and maybe figure out where to find Jack, the purloined poodle. After breakfast, of course.

CHAPTER 4

Wibbly-wobbly Time is the Best Time

Our Druids got up at dawn and went through their bizarre coffee making ritual. It was sure a lot of trouble to make some hot bitter water, and I can't imagine what kind of poor senses they must have if they think that stuff is any good, but coffee will just have to remain one of many human mysteries to us hounds. If there's anything good about the coffee making, though, it's a clear signal that food is coming right afterward. Atticus made us some pork sausage links topped with a light sausage gravy, and then he whipped up a couple of light vegetarian omelets for himself and Clever Girl.

These days Granuaile always had a book of Polish poetry in front of her by a lady named Wisława Szymborska. It had both the English and Polish versions side-by-side, and she was memorizing the Polish version so that she'd have a new headspace she could use for plane shifting. But during breakfast or whatever meal she was sharing with us—her schedule was unpredictable now since she spent a lot of time in Poland and the time zones were different—she often liked to share a few lines in English with us.

"Listen to this, you guys—it's from one of Szymborska's poems called "Dreams" and kind of applies to Druidry, though it's unintentional. Especially if you think of the flying bit as shifting planes. I'll give you the translation:

And we—unlike circus acrobats,
conjurers, wizards, and hypnotists—
can fly unfledged,
we light dark tunnels with our eyes,
we wax eloquent in unknown tongues,
talking not with just anyone, but with the dead."

She smiled at Atticus when she finished and he smiled back. "That's good stuff, even in translation."

It was. Both of our Druids were pretty happy these days. Granauile loved learning this language and its poetry, and Atticus loved not being chased by vampires anymore. He still had a lot of debt to pay off to mercenary yewmen, and he was no longer rich, but he said he had a plan to fix all that. "I know where all the gold is," he explained, "or at least I know elementals who do. It's just going to take me a bit of time to set things up to where I can extract it safely without giving Gaia a bunch of new problems, and I couldn't take the proper time during the vampire business." He was going to set up a claim in a barren desert in southern California and then say his gold came from there. When other humans went to start mines near the same place, they'd not hurt much because it was already a desert, plus they wouldn't find anything and be ruined by their own greed. That was his long-term plan, and he said he had a short-term plan too involving a treasure map, but he'd get to it later.

Granuaile had the day off from her bartending job in Poland, so she was going to lounge by the river, memorize Szymborska, and give Orlaith belly rubs. Atticus was going to drive me and Starbuck into Eugene so we could fight crime.

We were out the door and piling into the rental beast when Atticus's new phone rang. "Oh, good morning, Detective Ibarra," he said. "How can I help?"

Atticus put the detective on speaker so I could hear. "There's some serious confusion with the timeline of this case, and I was hoping you could clear it up," she said.

"I doubt it since I didn't really notice times—I don't wear a watch or check my phone obsessively—but I'll try."

"Great. Mr. Lumbergh, Mr. Goggins-Smythe, and Ms. Pierce all claim you first met them yesterday."

"Huh. That's fascinating."

"You also discovered the body of Ms. Boone-Sutcliffe."

"Right. I do remember that. We were both there. We exchanged cards."

"How is it possible for you to be in Eugene, then Bend, then Bellingham, and finally Portland all on the same day?"

"I'm not sure that it *is* possible. Is this a trick question?"

"No, it's a serious question. How were you able to visit these people on the same day?"

"I don't think I did."

"So when did you visit them?"

"In a sequence of time that's physically possible, of course. I think one or more of them must be mistaken about when they saw me. I'm sorry I can't be of more help. I try not to notice the passage of time. It stresses me out, releases cortisol into the bloodstream, shortens the life span, contributes to poor skin and many other undesirable effects. Better to just live in the present, whatever time it is."

"What time is it now, Mr. Molloy?"

"Are you trying to stress me out? It's between breakfast and lunch."

"I see. How long have you been an animal rights advocate?"

"For more than two millennia."

"Hmph," the detective grunted as if Atticus had made a joke. But I think maybe he had actually told her the truth there. I'm terrible at figuring out times for things and always get the terms messed up—like Doctor Who, I prefer to think of time as "wibbly-wobbly"—but I'm pretty sure that "millennia" is one of the longer measurements of time. Atticus *will* tell people the truth sometimes, confident that they won't believe him or even think he's being serious, and it's pretty funny to both of us when he does. Detective Ibarra continued, "Yet you just had that card you gave me made yesterday."

"Really? How do you know?"

"This phone you're using is a burner phone, also activated yesterday. So you couldn't have known the number to put on your card before then."

"Wow, you're an excellent detective."

"What else do you do, Mr. Molloy? I'm finding very little history on you and it raises suspicions."

"Owning a burner phone, even several of them, is not illegal."

"Of course not. It is, however, the legal method that many criminals use to disguise their movements and whereabouts."

"It's also one of many methods that law-abiding citizens use to protect their privacy from an intrusive government."

"Where are you now?"

"At my home about sixty miles from Eugene."

"You don't have a car registered in the state of Oregon."

"That's correct."

"So how did you get down there from Portland last night?"

"I rented a car. That's what I do when I absolutely need one. Most of the time I don't need a car."

"Ah, so you must work at home. That brings us back to the question of what you do when you are not finding murder victims in my jurisdiction."

"Lots of meditation, three different kinds of yoga, some gardening. The usual."

"I meant what do you do for income? How did you get the money to rent a car and buy a burner phone?"

"What does that matter? I do odd training jobs and get by."

"It matters because your story is inconsistent and your background is shady."

"Lots of people get elected to high offices that way. I should run for President."

A frustrated sigh blew through the phone. Instead of shouting at Atticus, the detective calmly changed the subject. "Where were you when Ms. Boone-Sutcliffe was killed?"

"I don't know. When was she killed—wait, you know what? It doesn't matter, because whenever it was, I was not in her house with a dart gun to kidnap her dog."

"I notice you have the dog."

"Which I did not kidnap. I took him with your permission and will return him to any family member of Ms. Boone-Sutcliffe as promised. He's doing much better, by the way. His stress levels are way down. How are yours?"

"Going up the longer we talk."

"Would you like to talk later, then?"

"No, I want you to stop obstructing my investigation and answer plainly."

"How can you say I'm obstructing? I found the body, gave you a motive for the killing, and gave you a pool of suspects that you can easily track down."

"You mean the regional dog trainers' forum? Useless. You have to be a member to post to the forum but anyone from the general public can view it and see who owns a Grand Champion."

"But the general public is not adept at crafting perfectly dosed snacks for other dogs, would not know that Mr. Lumbergh had four additional Brittany spaniels, or that Ms. Pierce had additional French bulldogs, and so on. The methodology suggests a trainer who knew the owners already."

"You're a trainer."

Atticus rolled his eyes. "Yes, but I didn't know anyone previously. I only met these people in the last few days. Or just yesterday if you want to believe in the impossible."

"That's fine, but your involvement in all this makes no sense."

"I like dogs and don't want to see them hurt. That's hardly uncommon."

"But traveling as much as you did over someone else's dogs is impractical, to say the least, without someone paying expenses. Is Mr. Goggins-Smythe paying you for your time to investigate this?"

"I sure hope so. I haven't sent him a bill yet."

"When I spoke to him he said he hadn't hired you in any official capacity but you told Ms. Pierce that he had."

"That's okay. We'll work it out."

"You also told him you knew Detective Callaghan in Eugene but I just finished speaking with Detective Callaghan and he's never heard of you."

"Well, he was pretty drunk at the time."

"Detective Callaghan's been sober for nine years now."

"Everyone's very proud of him, too! Ah, well, I guess I'll just have to reintroduce myself. It's been a long time and it's not his fault."

"You're saying you knew him when he was still drinking? Wouldn't you have been a child then?"

Atticus's eyes grew big, but I'm pretty sure nothing happened in his pants. I think it meant he was surprised because she'd caught him at something. Or at least appeared to. There's no way Atticus was a child nine years or days or centuries ago. I mean, he's older than railroads. Older than vampires. He's even older than Keith Richards! "I suppose technically I would have been," he said, "but I was precocious."

"You are entirely too glib, Mr. Molloy."

"Perhaps. But I'm also not the murderer. You're wasting time talking to me."

"Confirming statements and tracking down inconsistencies is part of the job. They often point to the solution. Not a waste at all."

"Fair enough. I'll let you get back to it, then, unless there's anything else."

"If you can't account for your whereabouts at the time of Ms. Boone-Sutcliffe's murder I'm afraid that will make you a person of interest."

"You still haven't told me when she was killed. I'm pretty sure it was long before I discovered the body and called 911."

"Two nights ago between midnight and three in the morning."

"I was at home, asleep."

"Can anyone confirm that?"

"My hound got a pretty good belly rub right before I went to bed. Made his leg kick out and everything, got him in that spot right beneath the last rib." Hey, yeah! I remember that! But I couldn't say so to the detective. I noticed he didn't volunteer Granuaile's name. He probably didn't want to get her involved.

"That is not a very good alibi, Mr. Molloy."

"I don't live my life in such a way as to provide rock solid alibis whenever some stranger dies unpredictably more than a hundred miles away from me. Do you have multiple witnesses watch you sleep every night, Detective Ibarra, just in case you become a person of interest in some random murder?"

"I see that you wish to remain uncooperative. Noted."

That finally annoyed Atticus. His expression and tone turned dark. "I note that you are trying to intimidate someone who has done more work to solve this crime than you have. Guess I'll just have to solve it on my own."

"Do not interfere with my investigation."

"You must have misheard me. I said I'm going to solve the crime. For my client."

"Mr. Goggins-Smythe is not your client!"

"I'll call you as soon as I've done your job for you." Atticus pressed his thumb on a button to end the call—marvelous things, thumbs—and he sighed. "See, Oberon? I told you the timeline was going to be a problem."

<What can you do, though? Just let me and Starbuck solve it like you said.>

"That's not exactly what I said…"

<I know, it's what you *meant* to say. That's okay, Atticus.>

"Let's go. We have to return this rental and see if we can catch up with those other two hound owners."

<We also need to get me one of those Sherlock hats and a pipe.>

"We do? Those are called deerstalker hats."

<Even better! I will stalk deer *and* criminals!>

"What kind of pipe do you want?"

<Whatever the esteemed Mr. Holmes used.>

Atticus pulled out onto the road and lowered the rear windows as a courtesy to me and Starbuck. "Well, in the original stories by Sir Arthur Conan Doyle it was a churchwarden pipe, but in films and stage productions the actors often used a calabash pipe."

<Hmm. Did Gandalf use either of those?>

"Yes, he used a churchwarden pipe to smoke Longbottom Leaf with Bilbo Baggins."

<That's what I want, then! The pipe of wizards and world-famous detectives!>

CHAPTER 5

A Man of Questionable Grooming Habits

stuck my head out the window and let my tongue flap around as we drove. The air tasted of pine and wild mushrooms and coming rain. The sky was gray instead of blue and we had the road almost entirely to ourselves until we got to Eugene. It didn't rain, though, it just kept threatening to like an impotent old guy who promises to kill you for pooping on his lawn, and that was fine with us.

We returned the rental and Atticus told me we'd shift around from now on since he had Starbuck figured out and would be able to save all his memories. He wasn't a complicated fella yet.

<But what about timeline worries?> I asked him.

"We're just heading up to Hillsboro. That's a conceivable trip for a morning's drive and the detective shouldn't have any problem with it if she feels like tracing my movements further."

Hillsboro smelled like grapes and hops. Maybe not all of it, but where we shifted in, it sure smelled that way. Atticus said it was home to a bunch of tech companies like Intel, and people called the area the Silicon Forest if they didn't want to call it Hillsboro, but for the record, I didn't smell any silicon.

Atticus had me and Starbuck on leashes for the sake of appearances, and we jogged to the home of Gordon Petrie, who didn't answer the doorbell. Atticus rang it twice and we were about to give up when I heard someone barking commands behind the house.

<Hey Atticus, do you hear that?>

No. What is it?

<There's somebody saying "Hup!" back there, like dog trainers do sometimes. Maybe he's in the backyard.>

"Worth a look," he said, and we scooted around to the side fence where Atticus could shout.

"Mr. Petrie? Are you back there? I need to discuss your Airedale terrier!"

The sounds of training ended and a couple of barks announced the approach of hounds, at least, if not the man himself. But he did arrive, though I couldn't see him over the fence. I just heard him ask Atticus, "Can I help you?" in a sort of tight, muted English accent, like he had lived with severe constipation all his life and hadn't heard about fiber. Atticus told him he was investigating a series of Grand Champion abductions and wanted to ask a few questions about his missing Airedale terrier.

"Yes. All right. Wait on the front porch, please. I'll be around in a moment."

As we walked back to the front I said, <This guy sounds like he hasn't laughed since Doc Brown invented the flux capacitor. What does he look like?>

Imagine a sausage, Atticus said after a pause.

<Yeah?>

But with all the flavor and joy sucked out of it. Just a tube of inert matter.

<What? How is that even possible?>

You'll see for yourself in a few moments.

I'm not the finest judge of human fashion, but you didn't have to be a genius to see that Gordon Petrie was trying to be normal and failing. As soon as he came through the front door I knew he was all kinds of wrong. First, he was wearing a type of pants that Atticus said were called *slacks,* and that's not something you should be wearing if you're training dogs. And if you're wearing them ironically then you should have some dog hair on them to demonstrate that you allow your hounds to touch you or that your hounds want to play, but Gordon's slacks were crisp and hairless. His shoes were the dressy black sort and highly polished. His long-sleeved white shirt was buttoned all the way to the top and at the wrists too. And a curious thin line of dark hair traced his jaw and formed a house shape around his mouth, the mustache part as strangely thin as the rest of it. Where had I seen that before? When I remembered, I had to warn my Druid.

<Atticus, he looks like Jafar! Watch out! Don't let him hypnotize you!>

Oh my gods, Oberon, don't make me laugh right now.

"May I ask how you heard of me, sir?" Gordon said.

"Absolutely," Atticus replied, pulling out one of his fake business cards and offering it to him. "I'm an animal rights advocate looking into this matter on behalf of Earnest Goggins-Smythe down in Eugene. His poodle was kidnapped like your Airedale and some others. There's been a rash of them in Oregon and Washington, and now someone's dead."

Gordon didn't even look at Atticus's card or move to take it. He quite purposely folded his arms across his chest. I was pretty sure that meant, in human terms, that he was being a dick. One that smelled like lemons and rubbing alcohol.

"Yes, I've heard about the passing of Verity Boone-Sutcliffe," he said.

"Oh?"

"Indeed. I got a call from a detective in Portland. She asked if you'd been to see me yet."

"Ah, that will save me some explanation then. Could you tell me if your other dogs were drugged with food or a tranquilizer dart?"

"With food during the night. They were unconscious when I found them in the morning." Atticus still held out his business card and Gordon's eyes flicked down to it and then back to Atticus. His nostrils flared.

<Atticus, why are you still trying to give him the card? He's not going to take it.>

I know, but keeping it in his face is making him uncomfortable.

"Look, let me save us both some time," Gordon said. "I'll tell you what I told the detective. Julia Garcia did it. She kidnapped all these dogs, reported hers stolen too, and then left town when she killed Verity. She's absolutely heinous and I hope she suffers in prison."

"All right...how do you know that for sure?"

"She lacks a moral compass and tries to undermine other trainers in competitions instead of training her client animals to a superlative standard."

"Okay, so you obviously bear a professional grudge against her, but do you have any proof she took your dog—what's his name, anyway?"

"His name is Queen Victoria Who Put Her Prince Albert in a Can."

<Whaaaaat? Was that his idea of a joke, Atticus?>

I think so because he's waiting for a reaction, but I'm not giving him one.

"And no, I haven't any proof," Gordon huffed once it was clear Atticus wasn't going to crack a smile. "Finding that is what detectives are for. I'm just sharing what I know, and what I know is that Julia Garcia is pure evil."

I chuffed in disbelief, and Gordon looked down at me and frowned as I shook my head at him. Who's he to call someone else pure evil when he grooms himself to look like a Disney villain? He opened his mouth to say something about me but Atticus didn't let him.

"Do you know if Julia has any other dogs besides the Grand Champion Italian greyhound?" he asked, and Gordon returned his gaze to Atticus, but noticed that the card was still hanging in the air between them.

"She used to have two others. I don't know if she still does."

"How do you know she's left town? She's in Tacoma."

"Detective Ibarra informed me and asked if I knew where she might be. The answer's no, I have no idea."

"Thanks for your time. Please call me if you think of anything else." Atticus thrust his business card right in front of Gordon's eyes and then dropped it, turning away. "Come on, hounds."

We trotted after him and Gordon said nothing, but I saw that he let the business card fall to the porch and he stepped on it like it was a spider.

<I don't trust that guy, Atticus.>

Me neither. And that goes for Starbuck too.

<You know what I think? I mean, yeah, maybe Julia Garcia is pure evil because we haven't met her yet, but we've met Gordon Petrie and he seems like the type to have a basement with lots of plastic sheeting on the walls and floors, you know what I mean?>

Yes, I do.

<The guy lacks a soul—did you see him? He probably thinks cauliflower is delicious! So I think it's more likely he's done all the kidnapping. You don't just go off on somebody like that. Or do you? What's the human perspective here?>

I bet that if you look into their past you will find that they either dated at one time or he asked Julia out and she rejected him. Something like that, anyway. He's behaving like he has a personal grudge against her, not a professional one.

<Yeah, okay, that makes sense. You know what doesn't make sense though? His remaining dogs. I mean, we heard them when you shouted for him in the backyard, but after that, nothing. Did you see what kind they were?"

No, I didn't.

<Well, look, I can't be sure, you know, but one of them sounded like a poodle to me. What if he has Jack and the rest of them right there in his backyard?>

Hmm. It's a long shot, but it would be best to check, wouldn't it?

<I think so.>

All right, I'll cast camouflage, shape-shift to an owl, and fly back there to take a look. Let's find a place for you and Starbuck to chill out while I do that.

Atticus tied us up, loosely, to an outdoor table in front of a coffee shop. Everyone would assume he was inside and would return soon. When no one was looking he winked out of sight, stripped, and put his clothes on the table. He dropped the camouflage off them when he was finished and asked me to guard them, then he shifted and hooted once before flying off.

Starbuck and I got petted a lot by people going in and out of the shop, and that made the time go by fast. It didn't seem that long, anyway, until I heard Atticus in my head in his slightly muffled animal voice.

<No poodles, Oberon. He's got two dogs he's training back here, both of them Kerry Blue terriers. Gorgeous hounds. Good idea to make sure and eliminate possibilities. Flying back now.>

<Huh. Trying to track down Julia Garcia would probably be a waste of time, wouldn't it? I mean since Detective Ibarra is already on it and says she's out of town.>

<That's a fair assessment.>

<So that means we probably have to start examining the people in the online forum, doesn't it? Look for a trainer who has veterinary experience, maybe.>

<Sounds like a solid plan to me. But if you don't mind, I'd like to meet up with Earnest and Algy in Eugene. I want to ask him about Verity's friends on the forum and see if we can get him to agree to hire me since I keep telling people he has.>

<Okay! I hope Algy feels like playing today.>

CHAPTER 6

The Brazen English Setter Maneuver

When we got to the dog park in Eugene, Atticus restored the batteries to his phones and called Earnest. Until Earnest got there, Atticus said, we could just enjoy ourselves. Starbuck and I did just that, playing around with a hyper yellow Labrador as a yappy little Pomeranian criticized us for having too much fun. Toy breeds were always like that since they didn't have legs long enough to do anything except jump into a human's lap and stay there.

Algernon showed up soon thereafter, in a much better mood than I saw him the first time, and he barreled right into us, and we had ourselves an old-fashioned dog pile, Starbuck mixing it up with the big dogs despite being less than half our size. Algy was a ton of fun to wrestle with now that he wasn't trying to rip my throat out. The Pomeranian was outraged that we dared to frolic and roughhouse so freely.

I did break it off pretty quickly, though, because I didn't want Earnest to worry and I also wanted to hear what Atticus was going to ask him. The other hounds weren't ready to quit, though. They thought I wanted to be chased and they were going to grant my wish. So when I disengaged and trotted over to Atticus and Earnest, they were nipping at my hind legs, and I had to speed up. That got us all running in circles around the humans as they talked, and holy angry badger balls, I had no idea how irritating Pomeranians could be when they got worked up like that one did.

Atticus was mostly just talking about finding Verity and Starbuck so I didn't miss anything. The yellow lab and the Pomeranian got called away by their owners after a few thousand laps so it was just me, Algy, and Starbuck, and we all took a break an equal distance away from each other, points in a triangle around our humans, to pant a bit and recover our strength, watching to see who would start the shenanigans again.

But it turned out not to be any of us. Well, maybe it was Starbuck. But really he was just reacting. Two English setters rocketed by us to go see the yellow Labrador, and Earnest said, "Hey, that's Mr. Darcy and Elizabeth." He looked over his shoulder and waved at a woman jogging toward us from the parking lot. It was the one who had stripes on her legs before, which she didn't have this time but I'm pretty sure she was still a Huguenot, whatever that was, and her hair still didn't match her eyebrows. "Hey there, Tracie."

"Hey guys!" she called from a distance.

While she caught up Earnest said in a lower tone to Atticus, "I hope you don't mind. I invited her along to hear what happened."

Atticus shrugged. "Not at all." And once Tracie got close enough to smell, Starbuck started barking his head off like that Pomeranian, except he was as unhinged as Imhotep's jaw in *The Mummy*. His lips peeled back and showed maximum teeth, and when a dog is genuinely angry you can hear it in their bark, too. It's the difference between a territorial "Hey, this is mine!" kind of thing versus "I will gnaw on your arm fat and chew on your cheek meat and bury you in my backyard if you get any closer!" Starbuck looked and sounded like he was going to latch onto her face any second and Tracie pulled up as Atticus hurried to calm him down.

"Whoa, whoa there, Starbuck," he said, kneeling down and looping a finger underneath his collar.

"Starbuck?" Tracie said.

"Yeah, you recognize him?"

"No, uh—" Starbuck was still barking ferociously so it was no wonder she hesitated. "Just a cool name, that's all."

"Sure you don't recognize him? He belonged to Verity in Portland."

"That's Verity's Boston terrier?"

"Yep." Atticus spoke to me via our mental link. *Oberon, Starbuck is positive that Tracie is the person who shot Verity and killed her, intentionally or not. He recognizes her scent. That's why he's going nucking futs.*

<Three kinds of cat shit! Should I tackle her?>

No! I trust Starbuck's nose but no human court will. We have to get proof so the human police can arrest her.

<How do we get proof?>

Well, she's probably going to leave so that Starbuck can calm down. You kind of trail after her and just listen in case she's upset and says something useful, and I'll try to think of what else we can do. If she kidnapped the other hounds, we need to find out where she's keeping them.

<Got it.>

Atticus got a firmer grasp on Starbuck and apologized to Tracie for his behavior. "I'm sorry," he half-shouted over the barking. "He's touchy like Algy was yesterday. Verity's dead, you know."

"She's *dead?*" Her hand flew to her mouth, which is what humans often do when they want to say "Oh, shit!" but don't think it's the right time. And maybe her surprise was real. She could have shot Verity in a panic that night, and left the house thinking she was only asleep and would wake up soon, no harm done.

"Yep," Atticus said. "Found in her home with a dart in her, just like the one Earnest found in Algy."

"Oh my God. But if it was a tranquilizer, how did that kill her?"

My Druid shrugged. "The autopsy's not back yet. But the police are certainly looking into these hound abductions a lot closer now that there's murder involved."

"Oh, God. This is terrible. I just…I have to go. I'm sorry. Poor Verity." Her eyes welled up and leaked and she turned away, walking back to the parking lot. She called for her hounds, who hardly had any time to play, and Earnest hollered that he would call her later.

Okay, buddy, you're up, Atticus said, staying put with Starbuck firmly in his grasp.

I started wagging my tail and pranced after her, and she didn't even notice because her English setters came running over, and she thought the footfalls were all theirs. She never even looked back to check—she just pulled out her phone and tapped at the screen a few times before putting it up to her ear. Her hounds were cool, and they sniffed at me as we walked, but I wasn't interested in them at the moment. Somebody picked up her call and I listened in to her side.

"Mary. Listen. You need to get rid of the poodle now— all of them, actually. Right away. They could connect me to something awful." There was a short pause and then she continued. "I don't want to say on the phone, but trust me, it's big trouble. So can you do it?" Her face scrunched up as she listened to the answer and I shot an update to Atticus.

<She's talking to someone named Mary on her phone and telling her to get rid of the poodle and the others!>

We need to track Mary down, then.

Tracie spoke again, wiping tears from her cheek. "Clive has him? Well when's he getting back?" She waited for a response and replied, "How late?"

Atticus whispered an idea in my head: *Oberon, if you can grab her phone without biting or scratching her at all and get it to me, we can find out who she's talking to and save the hounds.*

<Can I knock her down or just run into her?>

Yes. Make it look like an accident. You're going to take that phone like you're playing fetch or something.

<On it!>

"Well, have him do it as soon as he gets back. Don't wait until tomorrow," Tracie was saying.

I was glad to have the English setters on my ass right then because I—or rather Atticus—could blame what I was about to do on them. I spun and gave one of them a quick nip on the ear and barked once to get them riled up, then it was just two quick bounds to plow into the back of Tracie's legs and the fun began.

Humans are pretty easy to figure out if you want to take them down. Plant your paws in the middle of their back and they'll fall face first and put their arms out to break their fall.

I didn't want that because then she'd most likely be on top of her phone. But if you can make a human fall backward, and one or both of their arms are kind of raised from their sides, as Tracie's was with her phone to her ear, then the arms windmill in panic, going up in the air in a futile attempt to catch their balance before rotating down to find the ground before the back of their head does. When I swept her legs out and she toppled backward toward the ground with a "Whoop!" her conversation ended and reflexes took over. Her arms flew up and the phone sailed out of her hand in an arc—no, what's that math word?—parabola! Gotta remember to ask Atticus for a snack for that one. Her fingers splayed out behind her to take the impact, and she actually hit the ground on her backside before her phone did. It was in one of those plastic protector case thingies, a sensible precaution against drops, and I spun and leapt for it as her English setters came after me. I bowled right between them, scooped up the phone between my lips as a faint tinny voice said, "Tracie? What's happening?" and sprinted full speed away from there toward Atticus.

The English setters were all in now, woofing as they pelted after me, and that was perfect, because that's the first thing Tracie saw when she got to her feet. She couldn't say I was a bad dog when it looked like her own two hounds were responsible for the "accident."

"Damn it! Mr. Darcy! Elizabeth! Get back here!" she shouted.

<Incoming, Atticus! Going to just drop it and keep running,> I warned him. <Somebody named Clive has Jack the poodle right now and won't be back until tonight. Tracie told Mary to make Clive get rid of the hounds as soon as he gets there.>

Atticus was squatting down on the ground, still holding on to a supremely agitated Starbuck with his right hand. I angled my run so as to pass by on his left and let the phone fall from my mouth as I passed. He snatched it out of the air, and the English setters just churned on past, and since it looked like fun, Algernon barked and came along to see if he could catch up. Atticus gave me a play-by-play as I led a merry chase.

Eww, lots of slobber here. But still unlocked and working, good job. Let's see, end call, got the phone number, go to contacts…yep. There it is, Mary Yarbrough, address in Arkansas. Wow. Okay, bring the hounds back around and we'll go save the ones she kidnapped. You're on your way to a sirloin, buddy.

<Aye-aye, coming around, sir! And you said *sirloins* before, meaning more than one.>

I began to circle, the English setters baying behind me, and saw Atticus toss the phone to Earnest so he could return it to Tracie. Already her approach was sending Starbuck into new fits of anger.

"Sorry about that," Atticus called to her. "Hope you're all right. Your phone still works, apart from being a bit slobbery. Your call ended though."

She didn't reply, just scowled, snatched the phone from Earnest's hand and then glared in my direction. I halted, the English setters barked and wanted a tussle, but Tracie called them away, and they responded. She had their food, after all. Once they were out of range, I pawed at Algy a little bit to preserve the fiction that I was just a rambunctious hound without any crime-solving agenda, and he was happy to box with me. She could try to pick a fight, but Atticus would be all smooth and apologetic if she did. And besides, she clearly had other things on her mind, places to go, weapons to hide or destroy.

As she stalked away with her English setters, I trotted back to my Druid and Starbuck. <Atticus, if we have to prove she did it, we will probably need the murder weapon. How are we going to get that?>

We're not going to. We're going to sic the police on her while we go get the hounds in Arkansas. But I'm probably going to need to think ahead of how to handle all this without creating more timeline issues they can't ignore. Let me get Starbuck settled and say goodbye to Earnest, and then we'll get a move on.

Handling Earnest was done easily enough: Atticus told him he just thought of something that might lead him to Jack. "But I was wondering if you'd be willing to hire me for a dollar? Just so I can say you're my client, and I'm working on your behalf?"

Earnest blinked. "Sure. I mean, if you find Jack and bring him back, I'll pay you a thousand more."

"Great. We'll talk soon. And say, is Jack microchipped so that any vet could make a positive ID of him and who he belongs to?"

"Of course. That's standard practice now."

"Excellent."

I barked a farewell at Algy as Atticus, Starbuck, and I jogged to the rental car. He called Detective Ibarra in Portland as we pulled out of the parking lot.

"Hello, Detective! As promised, I've taken care of things. I'm now working for Earnest in earnest to find his poodle, and my investigation has unearthed some facts. I'm positive that Tracie Chasseur in Eugene is the one who killed Verity Boone-Sutcliffe," he said. "But she might be going home to try to hide or destroy the murder weapon even now. If you call Detective Callaghan and get him over there right away you might even catch her at it."

"What proof do you have?"

"I overheard her making a phone call to someone named Mary just now in the dog park." Of course he didn't overhear that—I did—and that might be a point of contention in any court case later, but he had to tell her something she would believe. He relayed that conversation, including Tracie's surprise at the news of Verity's death, which spurred her phone call, and pointed out that she was a member of the regional trainers' forum. She'd have access to any number of veterinarians who would give her tranquilizers as a trainer. He added that he'd be working on finding out who and where Mary was to recover the abducted hounds, even though he already knew that information.

"If I do find out where the hounds are, you might get a call from an associate of mine," he said, "or maybe an officer in that local jurisdiction. He'll drop my name. That way you can charge her for all those related crimes if you can't nail her with Verity's killing."

He had to repeat himself and spell the name of Chasseur, the eighteenth-century French Huguenot, and now that I knew she kidnapped hounds, I didn't think my full name should include any French bits anymore. And then I wondered why Algernon hadn't barked at her the way Starbuck had if she had been the one to kidnap Jack.

Avoiding that must have been why she decided to use a tranquilizer gun. Bring snacks to toss over the backyard fence and the dogs will be snuffling around and catch a whiff of whoever dropped them. Knock them out from a distance and they won't get a chance, and that would have been important to her if she knew that she'd see Algy at the dog park later while she was playing the sympathetic friend. And then I guess it worked so well—much faster than working through a digestive system—that she decided to use it on Starbuck. Except that caper didn't go as planned.

When Atticus ended his call I asked, <Who's this associate of yours who might be calling her?>

"It will be me on yet another phone using an assumed identity. Because if these hounds are in Arkansas and we shift there, Detective Ibarra is going to have her timeline issues again. So we'll go ahead and shift and find the hounds, then call the local authorities under a different name to get them taken care of and prove Chasseur's involvement in the crime."

<If they're in another state how does that prove she did it?>

"She just made a verifiable call to this person who has the hounds and told her to get rid of them."

<Heh! I already knew that, Atticus. I was just testing you.>

Atticus took us to a drugstore first to buy another phone, but most importantly to buy me and the Boston a big bag of beef jerky. He was going to feed that to us for lunch while he looked up a few quick things before we set out to save Jack and Ulysses and Queen Victoria Who Put Her Prince Albert in a Can.

CHAPTER 7

Never Scoff at a Bad Omen

A tticus made himself a peanut butter and fluff sandwich for lunch while charging up the new phone, then spent some time looking up phone numbers he might need where we were going—the local police, humane society, veterinarians, and steak houses. He carefully removed the batteries from all his phones before we shifted near the address he'd memorized from Tracie's contacts. I noticed right away that it was hotter and more humid than Oregon. I could tell we'd be panting pretty soon, which would make it harder to sneak up on people if we had any sneaking ahead of us.

My Druid didn't set off immediately; instead, he crouched down next to me while his hand lingered on the bound tree. He looked up at it with an expression I recognized, while

Starbuck snuffled around the base. Atticus gets sentimental about trees sometimes. He says they have their own kind of intelligence and are precious because they're bound to Gaia even more intimately than he is, the first and best expression of any elemental you care to name. Whenever he gets like this I've found that it's best to let him talk about it a bit.

<What kind of tree is this?> I asked him.

"It's a post oak," he replied, his voice soft. Still, it carried in the silent woods. We were up high, I could see, on a ridge somewhere. Clear blue sky above, with the tops of trees spread beneath us in an unbroken canopy and I couldn't see any human buildings at all. We must have a pretty good run ahead of us.

"I haven't been here in a long time," Atticus said, almost whispering, his voice tinged with regret. "This tree is almost done with its life but it was a mere sapling when I bound it. All the others near here that I bound have died, their tethers broken, nothing renewed by the Fae rangers. I'll have to bind a different one to Tír na nÓg if we want to revisit the area."

<Where are we, exactly?>

"Black Fork Mountain Wilderness in the state of Arkansas, near the Oklahoma border. We're on Black Fork Mountain right now. There are big cats around here, Oberon, and black bears too, so keep an ear and eye out."

<Bears? For real?> I began to scan the trees around us for alarming bearlike shapes.

"For real. This is the closest I could get to where we're going. About six or seven miles down the mountain, there's a town called Mena. The house we're looking for is on the outskirts, kind of all by itself."

<Why would they bring all the hounds there?>

"It's private, remote. And they can advertise their stud services to four different states from here. They can reach Hot Springs or Little Rock in a few hours, or go west to Tulsa and Oklahoma City, and even reach Dallas and Shreveport without too much trouble. That part of the conversation you heard where you said Clive wouldn't be back with Jack until tonight? They might have already taken him somewhere for stud service."

<Huh. So this is *A Cabin in the Woods* kind of deal? I suppose the house we're going to is on Haunted Canyon or Bloody Death Road or something ominous like that?>

"No, no, nothing like that."

Except I could tell it *was* something like that by the way he paused before answering.

<What's the name of the road it's on? And don't lie because I'll probably see the signs.>

Atticus sighed. "It's just a name, Oberon. You have to promise not to freak out."

<Why? Is it Demon Chihuahua Street or something?>

"It's called Big Bear Road."

<BIG BEAR ROAD? Atticus, that's the worst possible name ever! It's like the very definition of a bad omen!>

"It's just a coincidence. They didn't buy property there with the intention to warn off hound detectives and their Druids."

<Well just because they don't know who's pulling the strings of their fate doesn't mean I have to ignore it when I see it! I'm getting the message loud and clear! It's a death trap, Atticus! Those poor hounds are probably already bear breakfast!>

"Would it make you feel better if I contacted the elemental here and asked where the bears are?"

<And how many of them there are and if they're hungry and if they're sleeping and have they eaten Jack yet!>

He snorted and shook his head like he does when he thinks I'm being silly. "I'll find out what I can." While he was doing that I sampled the air and smelled nothing particularly bearish. A gentle breeze was all oak wood and leaves and the slightly bitter whiff of a saucy squirrel. Starbuck padded around and managed to wake up that squirrel, and once the squirrel chattered in outrage, the Boston barked back. When he learned enough words, I would have to remember to teach him Ezekiel 25:17 so we could do The Full Jules together someday.

Starbuck stopped barking abruptly and gave a little whimper instead, looking at my Druid. Atticus must have told him to be quiet.

"There's a bear nearby," he whispered. "He was asleep. Now he's not."

<It's the squirrel's fault!>

"Or maybe Starbuck's."

<The squirrel *made* him bark! The first rule of behavior in the animal kingdom is that squirrels are always wrong, Atticus!>

"It'll be fine. Or it should be. He's behind us. Let's just head straight down the mountain. No bears ahead. And both of you try to stay quiet and leave the squirrels alone."

We weren't running downhill but we weren't walking either. Starbuck and I took very quick breaks at some trees and picked up the scent of that bear. We peed on them because it was our joyful duty.

Atticus said it was the middle of the afternoon. Our drive into Eugene and assorted shenanigans had taken up most of the morning, and Arkansas was in a time zone ahead of Portland so we weren't terribly far away from sundown. Starbuck and I were panting halfway down because it was pretty hot, and Atticus had some sweat beading up on his face.

Once we got down to the bottom of the mountain the terrain was more of the rolling hilly sort populated by collections of leafy trees with human roads slashing through them.

Atticus stopped us at the edge of a green pasture while we were still shaded by trees ringing the edge of it. Off in the distance, I could see a low-slung house and some other human stuff, none of it looking particularly prosperous. Kind of junky, really. You could tell whoever lived there probably subsisted on cheap frozen burritos and cheesy pasta out of a box. Atticus said such humans were always in danger of getting scurvy because they never got enough fresh fruit and vegetables.

With such a nice pasture, you'd think they'd have a cow on it or maybe a goat or some sheep, but we didn't see so much as a chicken on it.

"Okay, that's it straight ahead. Still an hour before sundown. How are you guys doing?"

<I'm fine. For now, anyway. How's Starbuck?>

Atticus paused before answering, but then said, "He seems to be okay too. All right, I need you both to stay here." Atticus began taking off his clothes. "Guard my stuff again. I'm going to go scout things out. If the hounds are there and you're with me you might set them off to barking and I don't want that yet. I'll let you know what I'm up to through our mental link. Just lie down and rest up and we'll decide what to do soon."

He folded up his clothes and took out all of his phones and batteries. Two of them he left underneath his shirt, but he put the battery in the newest one and turned it on. Then he shape-shifted into a Great Horned Owl, which freaked out Starbuck a little bit since he wasn't in camouflage this time, and he flew off with his functional phone in his talons.

This was a good plan, because Atticus was silent when he flew as an owl, and it was unlikely that the hounds would sense him nearby right away. He's very smart for a human.

He circled the house a couple of times and then landed on the roof where we could see him from our spot at the edge of the pasture.

<I see the hounds,> his voice said into my head, but it sounded a little bit different since he was in animal form now. <There's a Brittany spaniel, an Airedale, a French bulldog, and an Italian greyhound. A couple of others too. All males, including Queen Victoria.>

<But no poodle?>

<No. Presumably Jack is with Clive, wherever they are.>

<Are they all okay?>

<Technically, yes. They don't look abused. But they're not happy either. They're kept separate in fenced-off areas on bare cement, sort of like a kennel or an animal shelter. They can't get out and roam around. They look pretty miserable.>

<Is anyone home?>

<Going to check in a moment. Going to call out the police first. Tell them these hounds are sought in connection with a murder in Portland and to contact Detective Graciela Ibarra about it. We need to get a vet with a chip reader out here to confirm these are the hounds we're looking for."

<Oh yeah! What name are you going to give them?>

<I'm thinking Scott Fitzgerald. Betting that they've never read *The Great Gatsby*.>

<Is that the story full of rich people where the woman adopts a dog and then she gets run over and we never find out what happens to the dog?>

<Yep, that's the one.>

<Worst book ever.>

Atticus shape-shifted back to his human form on top of the roof and scooped up his phone before it tumbled off. Naked guys on rooftops would normally inspire comment but we were in an isolated area surrounded by trees and mountains and no one saw him but us. He tapped in some numbers and talked for a while, and the sun kept sinking toward the horizon and the air began to cool down a little bit. Starbuck dozed off, but I was too interested in saving the hounds to do that. There were *sirloins* at stake here.

Atticus dropped the phone from his ear and his human voice said in my head, *All right. Police are informed and checking with Detective Ibarra and will be here eventually. In the meantime, I'll check out the house. I'm going in under camouflage. Circle around closer here, near the road, but stay under cover. If anyone drives up, let me know.*

<Got it,> I said, and turned to wake up Starbuck, but he abruptly snorted and looked up, no doubt in response to Atticus waking him up and explaining what to do next.

We crept along the edge of the pasture toward the poorly named Big Bear Road, trying to be as quiet as possible. You could say we were catlike, maybe, except without the tendency to meow and try to cover up our anal bombs in sand.

Atticus disappeared from the rooftop, no doubt in camouflage, and before we made it to the road he was giving me updates.

I'm inside now. There's a woman here, most likely Mary. Older than Tracie. Hasn't had a good life. Looks like she's having a rougher time of it than the hounds outside. Strong indications that Clive might be an abusive douchelord.

<So he's violent?>

Pretty sure, yeah.

<We can't let these hounds stay here. Let's bust them loose now!>

If we do that then we become the focus of the investigation. We just have to wait for the police to arrive and confirm these hounds all belong to someone else, which puts the blame on Clive and Mary and Tracie.

<Well what if Clive gets here, and Mary says he has to "get rid of them" before the police arrive?>

Then we will definitely do something.

<What if Mary called him already and told him to get rid of Jack?>

Then there's nothing we can do about that. Our best option right now is to wait.

<I hate waiting. I am like Inigo Montoya that way.>

I'm seeing some photos around the house, Atticus said. *A younger Mary with a younger Tracie. Looks like they're cousins, at least, but more likely sisters.*

<Ohhh. So Tracie was doing all this for her sister. Mary's having a difficult time with Clive, and the only thing Tracie could think of to help was to get her some humping money—>

Stud fees, Oberon. Let's use the proper term.

<Right, sorry. Because humans often fight about money. So maybe Tracie thought, hey, if I help Mary by giving her all this fee cash, then maybe Clive would be a nicer fella?>

She might have been thinking something along those lines, sure, Atticus said.

We settled down next to some oak trees and watched the road. Soon Atticus emerged from the house, dropped his camouflage, and shifted his form into a hound. This made both me and Starbuck very happy. We were just three hounds chilling out in the shade as the sun set, ready to protect the kidnapped hounds not far away. They were under a roof, which Atticus said was basically a large back porch.

When the sun finally bailed on us, the moon was almost full and very bright in a cloudless sky that looked like salt crystals floating on top of a rich beef broth. Nicer than Eugene, honestly, where it was all cloudy and a bit chilly.

Eventually, a distant rumble announced the approach of a vehicle of some kind, and I hoped it would be the police, but it turned out to be a big stinky truck, the kind you always see being advertised during football games where dudes with deep bass voices talk about torque and power and reliability and horsepower even though there are never any horses in the commercials. The headlights blinded us for a while until we blinked the glare away.

<That's probably Clive,> Atticus said in his animal voice, and I half-growled my response.

<Jack had better be okay.>

<Yes, indeed. Change of plan. When Clive lets Jack out of there, he's probably going to have him on a leash. I'm going to focus on getting Jack to join us for a run across the pasture. You knock Clive down, and Starbuck will nip his hand to make him let go of the leash.>

<That sounds great, but what about the other hounds?>

<We want to get Clive to chase us into the pasture. Jack will be safe and so will the hounds. We just have to delay until the cops get here.>

<Okay, I'm down with this.>

The truck passed by us, and Atticus rose from the ground, trailing after it. We followed, and once it parked outside the house and the motor choked and died, Atticus crouched down behind it. The other hounds could be heard barking now in response to the noise. They knew somebody was home and might pay attention to them.

<Okay, he might let Jack out of the driver's side or walk around to the passenger side. We'll have to wait and see,> he said.

That was a good call. Clive opened his driver's side door, and I could hear him say, "Stay there, damn it!" in a surly drawl. He was a tall, lanky sort, wearing bow-legged jeans, a dirty old trucker's hat pulled down over his hair, and cowboy boots crunching in the gravel of the road. He pulled out a cigarette and lit it, inviting toxins into his lungs and then puffing them out in white wispy clouds. Then he walked around to the passenger side, and we paced in tandem with Atticus that way, keeping well behind him and out of sight in the darkness, and once he turned the corner and his back was to us, heading to the passenger door, we slunk forward to close the distance.

Clive hauled open the door, blocking the exit with his body, and then reached in with a hand, searching for Jack's leash. Once he had it, he said, "Come on. Come on outta there," and opened the door wide. Jack hopped out, the paragon of poodles, all curly and proud and no doubt exhausted from being cooped up with Clive all day. As soon as Clive shut the door, Atticus gave the signal.

<Now!> he said. I leapt forward, not caring if Clive heard me, because there was absolutely nothing he could do to stop his imminent pratfall. He half-turned, putting all his weight on one leg as he pivoted, and that just made it easier to knock him down. He made a strangled cry in his throat, his cigarette

dropped out of his mouth as he saw me coming, and I'm pretty sure Starbuck missed his hand entirely because of all the flailing he was doing, but it didn't matter. He let go of Jack's leash in an attempt to deal with me. But I planted my front paws right in his chest and bore him down, noticing that he smelled like stale smoke and cheap whiskey, and then I trampled over him as we cleared the truck and turned left toward the pasture, his curses floating behind us like so much foul wind. And Jack was with us, happy to stretch his legs and be free, and it was so very good for about ten eons or so. But then Atticus had us stop and bark in the middle of the pasture, totally exposed.

<We want him to follow us,> he said. <Make some noise. I'm going to cast night vision on us to make sure we have an advantage.>

We barked and woofed until Atticus was satisfied. That was when he saw Clive coming after us with something like a staff cradled in his hands.

<Whoops! That's a shotgun! Not good!> Atticus said. <Let's keep heading for the trees, but keep barking!> We took off again, far faster than Clive Yarbrough and possessed of much better night vision, and he was shouting that he'd kill us all and feed us to his neighbor's hogs. I was glad that Starbuck and Jack couldn't understand him. Farther away I heard a woman's voice—Mary, I presume—shouting Clive's name, telling him to wait, she had to tell him something.

Since I knew what she had to tell him was to get rid of all the hounds, I was glad he didn't listen. Atticus's plan was working so far.

We got to the edge of the pasture and Atticus had us all stop and turn around to check on Clive, barking a few more times to encourage him to continue. He was kind of jogging with that shotgun now, which I'm pretty sure is against one of the rules, even if it's far below the one about not stealing my sausage and not putting mustard on it.

<All right, we're going to circle around to the left, put some distance between us, and not bark until we're out of range of his gun,> Atticus said. I thought that was a fine idea, right up there with pot roast and pork tenderloins.

I was about to tell him that when a noise behind me in the woods startled me and caused me to say instead, <What was that?>

They could all hear just as well as I could and we turned around at the same time, our noses quivering in the air. A grunt, a musky scent, and then a roar. It all added up to—

<A great big bear!> I shouted at Atticus.

<Yep! Run toward Clive!> he said, <I'll try to calm him down.> We scampered out of there as a black bear crashed after us, all teeth and claws and muscle. It must be the one that Starbuck awakened because of that squirrel. Since we'd invaded his territory and peed on it, he'd tracked us down the mountain. Running directly away from him toward Clive

seemed like a great idea until I remembered that Clive had a shotgun. And he was slowing down, raising it up to his shoulder, because he heard a whole lot of trouble coming his way.

<Angry man ahead! Angry bear behind!> I could feel its snorting breath on my backside. <Weren't you going to calm it down?>

<I'm trying! Make a sharp left turn now!> Atticus said, and we four hounds dodged left and kept running while the bear and Clive got closer. The bear was going to turn after us and roared again, but that put him close enough to Clive to make him shoot in panic. The pellets sprayed out and caught the bear broadside, but it was far enough away that it did little except make the bear rage out. We were forgotten, and Clive was the new target. He shot again, and it only provoked the bear further. Clive went down for the second time, the shotgun clattered away, and his high scream floated above the bear's roar.

<Oh gods, that didn't go as I planned,> Atticus said. <I have to get that bear out of here.>

I didn't know what Atticus had planned, but I quickly agreed with his bear removal initiative. <What did I tell you about this road? It's a bad omen!>

Two cars drove up said road and parked behind the big truck. Mary's voice sounded panicked now. "Clive? Clive! Answer me! Somebody's here!"

<Hold on,> Atticus said, bringing us to a halt a decent distance away. <I'll get the bear back in the woods and make sure he's okay later. I'd hoped to do that *before* he mauled anyone, but it's too late now.>

I imagine that he could have handled the bear more easily if Clive hadn't shot it, but eventually he convinced it to head back up the mountain and wait until he could see to its wounds, leaving a whimpering and well-shredded Clive Yarbrough bleeding in his own pasture.

The two cars, meanwhile, disgorged police officers and a veterinarian. They would have very little trouble finding where the hounds were kept since they were quite upset by all the noise they heard—especially the roaring bear.

Atticus coached us to move in closer to the holding area so we could see and hear what was going on without giving ourselves away in the darkness.

The police had a warrant to inspect the hounds only and see if they were the missing ones from the Pacific Northwest, but those shotgun blasts and the scream they heard gave them probable cause to do a whole lot more than that. They brought out flashlights and guns and fanned out into the pasture, finding Mary with no problem since she called for help and finding Clive soon after that. A whole bunch more police and an ambulance got called in as a result, but the veterinarian took that time to check those microchips and confirmed that all the hounds were stolen—even the extra ones we didn't know about. They belonged in Northern California.

<You know, Atticus, if you have Jack walk up to the vet now, he'll get back to Earnest along with the rest of the hounds, and I'll have earned my sirloins,> I said.

<You're right,> he admitted, and he made it so. Jack trotted right up to the vet in the light of the back porch and got his microchip scanned.

<We solved the case of the Purloined Poodle!> I said. <Starbuck and I make a great team!>

Atticus swung his hound face around to me and his ears pricked up. <You and Starbuck, eh?>

<Well, you helped a little, so maybe you can have a baked potato, but it was only because of us that you even knew something was wrong."

<That's true. I'm in the presence of investigatory genius.>

<You're damn skippy!>

CHAPTER 8

The New Holmes and Watson

A tticus retrieved his clothes and destroyed the burner phone for Scott Fitzgerald, who made his single call to the police and then vanished. We climbed back up the mountain and found the bear, which Atticus kept firm control of this time and even asked the elemental for help in healing him. He got all of the shot out of the bear, then asked the elemental to relocate him somewhere safe and far away, because he was sure that humans would come hunting him after what he did to Clive.

With that taken care of we shifted back to Oregon, and Atticus became Connor Molloy again, replacing his phone batteries and calling Detective Ibarra. She was a lot nicer to him this time because, despite his timeline issues, she had all the evidence she needed to clear the case off her books, and he had pointed her in the right direction—thanks to me and Starbuck, of course. Not that she never did anything— she found out that Julia Garcia's absence was an innocent visit with her family on the East Coast, for example, and yes, Julia and Gordon Petrie had a past together, but they had suffered a breakup so bad that she now had a restraining order against him.

Detective Callaghan had gone to Tracie Chasseur's house and found a dart gun—or a "projector", as they call it. Atticus showed me what they looked like online and it sure seemed like a gun to me, but you can buy most dart projectors without a license or background check.

They also found lots of veterinary gelatinous goo at her place that shouldn't be necessary for two healthy English setters. She tried to play it all off as normal and legal and their allegations as nonsense, until they told her they'd found the hounds in Arkansas, as well as ads for the stolen hounds' stud services online. Then everything became Clive's fault and she couldn't wait to confess. Atticus learned all of this when he went into the Eugene police station to give his statements that they would use in the trial, if there was even going to be one. It looked like they were trying to negotiate a plea instead.

Tracie said she'd only been trying to help her sister, Mary. Clive Yarbrough had lost his job a while back and slipped into alcoholism and meanness as a result. When he was drunk he liked to hit things, including his wife. Mary had cooked up an idea with Tracie to bring in some money through stud fees, the idea being that if Clive had money again and needed to drive the dogs around for their, uh…romantic rendezvous, he wouldn't drink as much and be nicer to her. The plan had only been partially successful. It had kept him out of the house and drinking a bit less, but he had traveled too far down the path of eternal asshattery and remained abusive.

Autopsy results reported that Verity Boone-Sutcliffe's heart had failed due to a dangerous drug interaction between her prescriptions and the tranquilizer. Shooting her had been a total accident, Tracie insisted. She'd been there for Starbuck and had been trying to draw a bead on him in the house when Verity surprised her in the kitchen and she fired in panic. Horrified at her mistake and worried that Verity might recognize her somehow from the forum, even though she was masked, she ran out of there before Verity even hit the floor. The district attorney was going to charge Tracie with manslaughter instead of murder, and then a bunch of lesser charges stemming from her hound-snatching spree.

Mary Yarbrough corroborated all of it, though she was going to face lesser charges like "possession of stolen property" and might get nothing more than probation. Clive was going to face those same charges once he got out of the hospital, but also domestic assault charges and a pretty mean divorce lawyer.

It didn't really matter to me: What mattered was that we had returned the Grand Champions to their humans for proper care and feeding. I asked what would happen to Tracie's English setters, so Atticus inquired. Tracie had no one at home to take care of them, so Mr. Lumbergh down in Bend offered to let them live with his pack of Brittany spaniels.

And since Verity Boone-Sutcliffe had no living relatives, Detective Ibarra was fine allowing Starbuck to stay with us until they could figure out what plans she might have made in her will.

To celebrate, Atticus cooked up some bacon-wrapped sirloins for me and Starbuck, then took us into Portland, where they have a real haberdashery that sells all kinds of hats, including deerstalkers. He bought me one, and a churchwarden pipe at another store, and then took us into a photography studio to get our portrait taken as a proper crime-fighting duo. Who's the new Holmes and Watson? Oberon and Starbuck, that's who.

EPILOGUE

When Atticus writes his books he always puts one of these things in there, so I guess I will too.

He told Granuaile he would be on the road for a few days, and she and Orlaith could just chill out in Poland if she'd like to for her work week. Atticus shifted us into Flagstaff, Arizona, where he shouldn't be anymore since the Flagstaff pack banished him, but we were there only long enough to rent a big SUV and drive south.

"I have to get some of my stuff before I leave Arizona for good," he explained, "and I'd like to clear my debts now that I have the time to do so."

He drove us to the Salt River near Mesa, where humans like to float on inner tubes down the river, drink beer, and get their skin burned by the sun. He parked off to one side of the road and hiked a short distance into the desert, where we were concealed by mesquite trees and creosote bushes and the occasional very nasty cholla cactus. He squatted down and spoke to the elemental, Sonora, and the earth parted in front of us to reveal what looked like an iron coffin.

"My rare books are in there," he reminded me. "And a treasure map."

<You mean like an X-marks-the-spot kind of map, and here be monsters, and all of that?>

"There's an *x*, I think, but none of the rest of it. And it's in an old version of Spanish."

<Are we going to go find the treasure?>

"Yes, we are."

<Awesome!>

This was a treasure map made by somebody named Sotomayor, who was with Coronado on some expedition long ago, and while on a side trip out of Coronado's vision, Sotomayor's group found a huge cache of Aztec gold that had been shipped up north purposely to be hidden from the Spanish invading Tenochtitlan. They planned to come back and get it later, cutting Coronado out of the deal, but never did. And Atticus had left it there all this time to see if someone else would discover it, since he really hadn't needed the money. Now he would use it to pay off his debts to the yewmen who had helped him against the vampires.

Tracking down the treasure wasn't nearly as exciting as I thought it would be. We just drove north once he had his books all loaded up, and then Atticus had the elemental help him find the gold and bring it to the surface.

It sure was shiny. Most of it went straight to Brighid, First Among the Fae, who then paid off the yewmen on his behalf, and he was free and clear and had some left over besides. He was going to unbind the remaining gold from its finished shape and rebind it with some rocks and minerals out in California to make it seem like he dug it out of the ground there.

So it was a long but happy road trip back to Oregon through California with our precious cargo of books and gold. Starbuck and I hung our heads out the window and made plans to fight more crime, bring an end to the villainy of squirrels, and eat more steaks. The future was all gravy as far as we could see.

The End

ACKNOWLEDGEMENTS

I want to thank Deborah Flynn-Hanrahan for showing me all the spiffy things in Portland. Should you wish to follow Atticus and Oberon's path through the city to Verity's house, you can pretty much do so starting at Peninsula Park. Random Order Pie Bar is a real place, and across the street from it, just a few doors down (at least at the time of this writing), is a café simply called Barista where Atticus got his flat white. And the houses in the Irvington neighborhood are really worth a look.

I owe a great debt to Sir Arthur Conan Doyle for inventing the world's most famous detective, to whoever came up with Boston terriers, and to Delilah S. Dawson for platypus puns.